SASQUATCH

Roland Smith

HYPERION PAPERBACKS FOR CHILDREN
New York

First Hyperion Paperback Edition 1999

15 17 19 20 18 16 14

This book is set in 13.5-pt. Adobe Garamond.

Library of Congress Cataloging-in-Publication Data
Smith, Roland.
Sasquatch / by Roland Smith.
p. cm.
Summary: Thirteen-year-old Dylan follows his father into the woods
on the slopes of Mount Saint Helens, which is on the brink
of another eruption, in an attempt to protect the resident
Sasquatch from ruthless hunters.
ISBN 0-7868-0368-1 (hardcover)—ISBN 0-7868-2315-1 (library)
ISBN 0-7868-1334-2 (paperback)
[1. Sasquatch-Fiction. 2. Saint Helens, Mount (Wash.)-Fiction. 3. Volcanos-
Fiction.] I. Title.
PZ7.S65766Sas 1998
Fic]-dc21   97-39650
J689-1817-1-10035

This book is for my wonderful agent, Barbara Kouts, who accompanied me on the first Sasquatch expedition, Kristen Behrens, who believed in the story the first time she heard it, and my wife, Marie, because all my stories are for her.

—R. S.

BEFORE . . .

AS FAR AS I KNEW, Dad had never been hunting. In fact, I don't think he had ever fired a gun. So, I was pretty surprised when he came home one afternoon with our minivan full of hunting gear and started spreading it out on the garage floor. Sleeping bag, tent, Coleman lantern and stove, playing cards, two cases of beer, compass, maps, deer body bag, binoculars, long johns, rifle, cartridges, scope, down vest, leather boots, sheath knife, and a couple packages of cigars. Dad doesn't smoke.

"I'm going hunting," he announced.

"Sure looks like it," I said.

Mom came out in her jogging outfit and stared at the stuff on the floor. "Looks like Christmas," she said to him. "For you."

"I'm going hunting," he repeated.

"With whom?"

"Some of the guys at the office invited me. They go every year."

"How many of them come back?" Mom asked and jogged off before he could answer.

Dad is not exactly the outdoor type. When we go on vacation we stay in hotels and eat in restaurants. His idea of a barbecue is to cook hamburgers on the stove in the kitchen, then take them into the backyard to eat them. His parents named him Bill Hickock after "wild" Bill Hickock of the Old West, but the only thing wild about Dad is his mind. Mom calls him "mild" Bill Hickock. Up until the hunting trip the name fit him pretty well.

"Where are you going hunting?" I asked.

"Mount Saint Helens."

That's comforting, I thought. He's going hunting on the slopes of an active volcano. We were studying volcanoes at school. Mount Saint Helens had erupted eighteen years ago and it was acting up again. Volcanologists said it could blow any time. "How long will you be gone?" I asked.

"We'll be back on Monday. Give me a hand."

He started moving the end of a workbench away from the wall. I took the other end and helped him carry it to the other side of the garage.

"That ought to be enough room," he said.

"For what?"

"The freezer," he said.

"Huh?"

"For the deer."

"Oh."

"They'll deliver the freezer tomorrow. You'll need to show them where it goes."

"You won't be here?"

"I'm leaving in about forty-five minutes."

He took the price tags off the gear, loaded everything back into the minivan, said good-bye to Mom when she got back from her run, and drove away.

The next afternoon a delivery truck showed up with the huge freezer. It opened from the top like a coffin and came with a set of keys to lock it, which I hung on a nail above the lid.

That weekend I goofed around with friends, watched TV, and did my homework, but during all of these activities I kept wondering what Dad was doing in the wilderness, or more accurately, what the wilderness was doing to Dad. It was hard to imagine him with a cigar plugged into his mouth, sighting a deer through his rifle scope, squeezing the trigger, then slitting the deer open and pulling its guts out. He was probably sitting in camp, keeping the coffee warm and playing solitaire while his buddies were out trying to blast Bambi.

I expected him to be back by the time I got home from school on Monday, but he wasn't. And he still wasn't there when Mom got home from her classes at Portland State University. I knew she was just as worried about him as I was, but she tried not to show it. Then, at about eight o'clock, the minivan pulled into the driveway and Dad walked into the kitchen. He looked like he had just returned from the front line of a war zone—he was unshaven, had ugly dark circles under his eyes, his clothes were ripped, and he had scratches all over his face and hands. Mom and I were speechless, but he wasn't.

"How late is the library open?" he asked.

That was last fall when I was thirteen. I'm fourteen now and it's spring. A lot has happened between then and now. For one thing Mom is in Egypt, but before I get into all that I better explain who I am.

My name is Dylan Hickock and at the moment I'm in my bedroom sitting in front of my computer, tapping away.

Mom thinks this whole thing started with the hunting trip, but I think it started in our garage years before I was born. The garage is Dad's nest. It's where all of his crazy ideas incubate and hatch.

In the 1970s Dad became an authorized typewriter repairman. He set up shop in the garage, and for about a year things went pretty well. Then the personal computer came along. Luckily for my parents, Mom had a good job at the time or they probably would have starved to death and I wouldn't be here.

Dad finally gave up on the typewriter-repair business after a year of sitting in the garage saying, *"These computers are just a fad. You wait and see—people are going to come back to the typewriter . . ."*

While he was waiting for the typewriter to make a comeback, a friend of his talked him into getting his real-estate license and Dad started buying and selling houses. This was not his life-long ambition, but he was good at it and it paid a lot better than sitting in the garage watching his typewriters collect dust.

By the time I was born Dad owned dozens of rental houses and the real-estate agency he once worked for. My parents weren't rich, but they had enough money for Mom to quit her job to take care of me full-time. When I was ten, and had figured out how to use the microwave without burning the house down, she went back to school to get her Ph.D. in Archeology. This doctorate thing was all Dad's fault. When I was nine he took us to see the King Tutankhamen exhibit and that was it—Mom was smitten by the ancient pharaohs. I started calling her *Mummy* instead of Mommy.

The parent switch worked out pretty well, because by then Dad spent most of his time hanging around home. All he had to do was put on his suit and tie a couple times a week and go over to his real estate agency. The rest of the time he hung out with me, fixed plugged drains and toilets at his rental houses, or tinkered around in the garage.

When he wasn't tinkering with machines, he was tinkering with ideas. He had a recliner in the corner of the garage where he would read for hours. If he got really fascinated by something he would sit at the workbench and type notes on one of his manual typewriters. I have a friend Doug Groves whose father does the same thing. But Doug's dad is an author and eventually the notes turn into books. Dad puts his notes in boxes, and as far as I know, never looks at them again.

You could never tell what was going to interest Dad. He would pick a subject like the Lewis and Clark expedition and read dozens of books about it. When his curiosity was satisfied, he would dive into another subject like astronomy or the sinking of the Titanic and he would be off again. If I wanted to know what Dad was up to, all I had to do was check out the titles of the books he had strewn around the garage.

When Mom went back to school, Dad and I made a deal with each other. For the next four years, while she was in school, she didn't have to be my mother or his wife. He and I would clean the house, cook our own meals, and not bug her.

Mom had only one requirement left to get her doctorate in Archaeology. She had to work on a dig in Egypt. We were all excited about the trip. I was excited because when she got back my mom would have more time to be my mom. Dad was excited, because he gets excited about everything. To help her prepare for the change in climate he built a sauna in the basement and bought her a tanning bed so she wouldn't be incinerated by the Egyptian sun.

When Dad returned from his hunting adventure, Mom's trip to Egypt was four months away. Instead of going to the library that night, he went to sleep. He was usually up and tinkering before I dragged myself out of bed, but the next morning when I left for school he was still asleep. When I got home from school he was in the garage. I expected him to be buried in books, but instead he was at the workbench trying to fix a garbage disposal from the kitchen of one of his rental houses. The sleep looked as if it had done him some good, but he still had scratches on his face and hands.

"I should just go out and buy a new one," he said,

referring to the disposal, which was in about a thousand pieces.

"So, how was the hunting trip?" I asked.

He shook his head. "Not much fun."

I glanced at the freezer. "Did you shoot a deer?"

He shook his head again.

"Did you see a deer?"

"No."

"Why did you want to go to the library last night?"

"Oh that . . ." He started to fit a couple of parts together. "I was so exhausted I didn't know what I was saying."

And I think that was the first time Dad had ever intentionally lied to me.

PART ONE

THE MONSTER

*There were giants in the
earth in those days . . .*
—Genesis 6:4

CHAPTER 1

FOR THE NEXT FOUR MONTHS Dad was on his best behavior and the hunting trip was not mentioned again. He spent more time than usual at his real-estate agency, worked on his rentals, and did not tinker with any new ideas. I should have realized this seemingly normal behavior was totally abnormal for him. The only excuse I have for missing this is that I was busy with school, friends, and the swim team. I simply wasn't paying much attention to my parents at the time.

The day finally arrived for Mom to leave for Egypt. Dad dropped us in front of the airport with her bags.

"I'll park the van and meet you at the ticket counter," he said.

I could tell Mom was nervous. This was her first trip out of the country, and it would be her longest period away from us. She was going to be gone for five months. Even though I hadn't seen a lot of her lately, I was really going to miss her.

As we stood in line with her bags, she ran down a list of things I needed to watch out for while she was gone. "You need to remind your father to do the shopping," she said. "And make sure you give him plenty of warning if there are any school events he has to go to or a swim meet. And you have all my numbers, but there are times when I'll be in the field and it will be difficult to reach me. Also, remind your father to take my Bug into the mechanic. I might as well have the problems fixed while I'm gone." Mom loved her red Volkswagen Bug. "And remember the time difference. When it's noon here it's 10 P.M. in Egypt. At least I think . . ."

"We'll be fine, Mom. We've had a lot of practice taking care of ourselves. The only thing you should be worrying about is getting your work done so we can call you Doctor Mom."

She started to cry.

"You've both been so wonderful . . . I would have never been able to do this without your help. It was crazy to start it in the first place, but now it looks like my dream is going to come true because of you and your father."

"Just don't open up a tomb with a curse on it," I told her, trying to lighten things up a bit.

"You know there are times when your father gets sort of distracted," she said.

No kidding, I thought.

"He's been very good lately," she continued. "But if he starts tinkering with something, you'll have to remind him that he has a son and other responsibilities to take care of. I won't be there to nudge him back to reality."

"No problem."

She wanted to say more, but thankfully it was her turn to check her bags.

Dad showed up just as we were leaving the ticket counter. "We're late," he said.

We hurried to the gate and got there just as the flight was starting to board. Dad laid a big kiss on Mom's lips, and I gave her a junior version. When she got in line she began crying again and disappeared down the passageway leading to the airplane.

Dad turned to me. "Do you want to watch it take off?"

"Nah." I was too old for that.

"Maybe we should stop on the way home, get some pizza, and eat to your mom's success."

Sometimes Dad came up with great ideas. We were weaving our way through the crowded corridor when Dad came to a sudden stop. He reached into his pockets and felt around. At first I thought he had locked his keys in the minivan. It would not have been the first time. But when I saw his face I knew it was something else. He was staring at a bank of newspaper dispensers and he had the strangest expression—surprise and fear with a little excitement thrown in.

"What's the matter?" I asked.

"I can't believe it! Do you have a couple quarters?"

"I think so." I rummaged through my pockets and came out with a handful of change. He picked out two quarters among the lint, sunflower shells, and other debris. "What do you . . ."

"Newspaper." He walked over to one of the dispensers lining the wall. Dad never read the newspaper. He said it was too depressing and the oversimplified stories caused more harm than good.

He came back with a paper folded up under his arm.

"What's going on, Dad?"

"We need to make a stop on the way home."

"I know," I said. "Pizza."

"Oh, yeah," he said. "That, too."

We drove over to North Portland and stopped outside an old church. There were a number of cars parked along the curb.

"What are we doing here?" My parents had taken me to church maybe a dozen times and it certainly wasn't this church.

"It's a meeting," he said. "I'll tell you about it later. Right now I want to get inside so we can find a good seat."

I followed him up the concrete path and through the thick oak doors. As soon as my eyes adjusted to the dim light inside it became clear that this was definitely not a worship service. There were about two hundred people in the church. Some sat on the pews and others stood in the aisles talking to each other. All three local television stations were on hand to film whatever was going to happen there. A few of the people were dressed up, but most of the crowd were wearing jeans. We sat down on the end of the last pew—the only seats available. I looked at Dad, hoping he would now give me some explanation about why we were here, but he was too busy looking at the crowd to pay any attention to me. A few people nodded at him as if they knew him.

At the front of the church, next to the pulpit, was a large white screen. A slide projector was set up a few feet down the aisle. A group of men and women were gathered around the projector and they seemed to be arguing, but we were too far away to hear what they were saying. The largest man in the group walked up to the pulpit and tapped the microphone to see if it was on. He had long black hair pulled back into a ponytail, and a shaggy beard that hung down over his broad chest. He was at least six feet four and wore jeans and a flannel shirt with a down vest over it. He had to weigh well over three hundred pounds. He swept away the sweat on his face with his hand

and wiped it on his jeans. It wasn't that hot in the church.

"Please take your seats!" he boomed over the microphone. "We need to get started here."

A few people sat down and others found spots along the walls to lean against. The big man waited for everyone to get settled.

"My name is Joe West," he began, his voice quivering a little, as if he were nervous. "I'm the president of B.F.I. We usually have about twenty people show up to our monthly meeting. I guess most of you are here because of the article that appeared on the front page of the newspaper this evening."

So that's what lured Dad here.

"For you new folks I want to tell you that you're welcome to join B.F.I. The yearly dues entitle you to our monthly newsletter and discounts on selected items from our mail order catalog. There's a sign-up sheet in the back.

"We were supposed to have two speakers tonight, but I'm afraid that our cryptozoologist, Dr. Theodore Flagg, missed his connecting flight from Denver and won't be arriving until tomorrow morning at the earliest. We'll reschedule his talk later this week. If you want to find out when, you can call me and I'll let you know."

"What's a cryptozoologist?" I whispered. "What's B.F.I.?"

"I'll tell you later," Dad said without taking his eyes off the pulpit.

"Our main event will still go on though," Joe continued. "It's a slide presentation by Clyde Smithers, one of our longtime members. And I'm sure that's why a lot of you are here tonight. Before he begins, Clyde has asked me to make an announcement. When he shows his slides he wants all the news cameras shut off; and no still photographs, please. I'm sure you newspeople can understand this. Clyde went to a lot of trouble to get the photos he's going to show you tonight and he doesn't want them broadcast all over the world without being paid for them. If you're interested in buying the rights to show the photos you can talk to him about . . ."

"My lawyer!" someone shouted from the front row. "You can talk to my lawyer about buying the rights to the photos." A skinny man about thirty years old stood up and faced the audience. "He's right here with me." He pointed to an older man with gray hair and a three piece suit sitting next to him. "His name is William Bly and he has all the paperwork."

"Thank you, Clyde," Joe said.

"One more thing," Clyde said. "My brothers are posted next to you camera people in case you forget to turn your camera off in the excitement. My brothers are there to remind you, as a courtesy to me."

Everyone laughed except the newspeople. Clyde's brothers were easy to pick out, they looked *exactly* like him with the same scraggly beards and thinning hair.

"Triplets," Dad said, before I could ask.

Clyde stepped up to the pulpit. "The following photographs were taken ten days ago. I'm not going to tell you where I took them for obvious reasons. You can turn the lights off now, Joe."

The church went dark and the crowd got very quiet. I looked at Dad. He stared intently at the blank screen and seemed to be holding his breath.

Click. The face of a gorilla appeared on the screen. At least that's what I thought it was. There was a collective gasp from the audience.

"Our old friend," Clyde said.

Click. The next picture was a full-body shot, and I realized that it wasn't a gorilla. The hair on its body was longer than a gorilla's and light brown, not black. Also, the animal had a dead deer draped over its shoulder.

"To give you an idea of the size of this cryptid, you might notice the deer he's carrying is a six-point buck. Now, maybe Joe could heft a two-hundred-pound deer on his shoulder, but I doubt he could do this . . ."

Click. The animal had turned around and appeared to be running up a very steep, rocky slope with the deer still slung over its shoulder.

"These photographs don't do justice to the speed he was moving up that talus slope. I wish I had my video camera. He ran up that hill faster than the deer could have when it was alive."

Click. The animal became smaller as it ran up the hill.

Click. Smaller still.

Click. It faded into a line of trees at the top of hill.

The lights came back on. No one said a word. I looked at Dad. He was staring straight ahead at the blank screen. A tear rolled down his cheek. I wanted to ask him what was going on, but it was so quiet in the church right then that everyone would have heard me.

Clyde walked down the aisle and retrieved his six slides from the projector, then walked back up to the pulpit. "Questions?"

A man stood up in front of us. "Where did you say you took these shots, Clyde?"

Clyde smiled. "Nice try, Frank. I didn't say and I'm not going to say." The crowd laughed. "Not just yet anyway. My brothers and I want to go back up there and we don't want the area contaminated."

A woman stood up. "The photos could be fake. It wouldn't be the first time."

"You're right," Clyde said. "They could be and it wouldn't be the first time. But I didn't fake them. They are as real as you are, ma'am."

More laughter.

Dad stood up. "Did you follow him, Clyde?"

"Glad to see you, Bill," Clyde said. "Yes, but it took me a half an hour to get to the tree line and I nearly broke my leg a dozen times scrambling over those rocks. He covered the same distance in less than five minutes. By the time I got to the top, the Sasquatch was long gone."

I stared at Dad. *Sasquatch. Bigfoot. How late is the library open*? I thought. Somehow this was all connected to the hunting trip.

CHAPTER 2

"LET'S GO," Dad said.

"Why?" The meeting was just getting interesting.

"You've got school tomorrow and I've heard enough."

It was only nine o'clock. I wanted to argue with him, but the look on his face convinced me not to. On the way out I glanced at the mail order catalog on the table. Across the top it said BIGFOOT INTERNATIONAL, which answered my question about what B.F.I. meant, but I had a lot more questions than this one.

"What's going on?" I asked when we got outside.

"A number of things," Dad said, unlocking the minivan. "But I need to sort it all out before I talk to you about it. Give me a little time."

This wasn't easy to do. I wanted to know what a cryptozoologist was and why he had cried when he saw the slides. We sped along the freeway in silence. Instead of taking our regular exit, Dad took the Wilsonville exit and stopped at his office.

"I have to pick up a few things," he said. "I'll be right back."

I waited in the van wondering about Dad's interest in Bigfoot. It wasn't like him to keep his tinkering to himself. I got out of the car and walked into his private office.

Things became a little clearer when I got inside. His usually spotless office looked like our garage now. The walls were covered with topographical maps marked with colored pushpins. Stacks of books and piles of magazines were strewn all over the desk and floor. The books had titles like, *Do Abominable Snowmen of America Really Exist?*, *The Lochness Monster*, *Encounters with Bigfoot*, *Field Guide to Sasquatch*, and *Where Bigfoot Walks*.

It wasn't exactly the kind of office that would inspire a buyer to purchase a home, which led me to the brilliant conclusion that Dad had not been coming into the office for the past four months to sell homes. He had simply moved his tinkering from the garage to his office so Mom would be able to take off for Egypt without worrying about us. If she knew about this she would fly home on the back of an Egyptian vulture—if that were the only way she could get here.

Dad looked pretty uncomfortable when I walked in on him. "I know all this is probably a shock, Dylan."

"You've got that right."

I picked up a journal called *Cryptozoology*—that word again.

"Cryptozoology is the study of animals that are believed to exist, but can't be proven to exist," he said. "They call the animals cryptids."

"And you're a member of Bigfoot International?"

"Not a real active member."

"You set up shop here so you wouldn't worry Mom."

He nodded. "I didn't want to ruin her trip."

"There wouldn't have been a trip if she knew about this."

"That's what I meant."

He had done an excellent job of concealing this new insanity, which made me wonder what else he had kept from me over the years. I thought I was able to read Dad pretty well, but I would never have guessed that he was into any of this.

"Do your employees know what you're up to in here?"

He laughed. "No way! They'd think I had lost my mind."

At least he was aware of how crazy this all looked. "What do they think you're doing in here all day?"

"They don't seem to care as long as I don't bother them. Although, they have been a little uncomfortable about me hanging around here as much as I have. But I guess that will end tonight."

I was relieved. Maybe the meeting had put a stop to his tinkering with Bigfoot.

"Now that your mom's gone," he continued, "I can move all this stuff to the garage and use that as a base of operation."

This did not sound like he was finished tinkering. "What's this all about, Dad?"

He sat down in his desk chair. "It's a long story, Dylan."

I took a wild guess. "The hunting trip?"

"That's where it started."

"You think you saw Bigfoot."

"I prefer the Native American name, Sasquatch," he said. "And I saw something. I wasn't sure what it was until tonight."

"Clyde Smither's photos."

"Right. And I know exactly where Clyde took those photos." He walked over to one of the maps of Mount Saint Helens and pointed to an X he had marked in red. "I rolled down that same talus slope four months ago."

*   *   *

It was eleven o'clock by the time we had all the stuff loaded into the minivan. As soon as we got the boxes into our garage at home, Dad started sorting through them and setting up his base of operations.

I went into the house and made a sandwich. The

pizza stop had vanished somewhere between the airport and the church. When I finished eating I thought about going back into the garage to see what Dad was up to, but decided against it. I was tired and needed time alone to think about how to handle his new craziness. I went up to my room and got ready for bed. As I lay there I thought about Mom sitting in the airplane. She was excited about her trip, but I'm sure she was also worrying about us. If I let her know about Dad's Sasquatch tinkering, the ancient Egyptians would be safe in their tombs for another few centuries, so that option was out. It was up to me to make sure he didn't get too carried away, but I also knew I might be too late to do anything about it.

Dad hadn't told me much about his close encounter in the wilderness. He said that he had climbed to the top of the hill looking for a deer. When he got there he saw a giant apelike creature and was so scared he fell over backward and rolled down the hill.

"I must have gotten knocked out in the fall," he said. "Because I don't remember anything after that. When I came to, I was lying on a bed made out of small fir boughs under a shelter made of thick fir branches. It was raining, but I was dry."

"Who made the shelter for you?"

"I don't know. And I don't know how I got to the shelter. It was at least two hundred yards from the hillside."

After he came to, he stumbled back into camp and asked his friends if they had put him in the shelter. They thought he had been drinking. He didn't tell them about seeing Sasquatch. Soon after he got back, he started going to the monthly B.F.I. meetings.

There was no point in trying to sleep with all this cryptid stuff bumping around in my brain. I got back out of bed and turned on my computer to see if I could find anything about Sasquatch on the Web. I had E-mail from my friend Doug Groves. He wanted to know if Mom had gotten off to Egypt okay. I wrote him back but didn't mention one word about the Sasquatch, then typed BIGFOOT into the search engine. Dozens of sites appeared on the screen. This was one place I was sure Dad had not looked for information. He was still a little bitter about the computer putting him out of the typewriter business so he refused to learn how to use one.

The first thing I learned was that Dad was not alone in his belief that undiscovered animals crawled, walked, and swam in wild places. I read about the bloodred Mongolian death worm, which is thought to live beneath the sands of the Gobi desert, popping up every once in a while to squirt deadly venom at predators.

In the Amazon rainforest of Brazil there was supposed to be a large animal that walks on its hind legs and eats small trees. Some people call it the Amazonian Bigfoot, but scientists say it's not a primate, but a giant sloth that was supposed to have gone extinct 8,500 years ago.

In the Congo they were looking for an aquatic dinosaur called the Mokele-mbembe. And off the coast of British Columbia there was another sea serpent called the Cadborosaurus, said to be similar to the mythic Loch Ness monster of Scotland.

But the prize cryptid was a giant apelike or human-like animal. Almost every country in the world had rumors of some type of giant primate running around the wilderness. The Abominable Snowman, or Yeti, was said to live in the Himalayan mountains of India, Nepal, and Tibet. In Mongolia nomadic tribesmen spoke of an animal called the Alma. In Tanzania there was an animal called the Agogwe. In Burma they had the Tok or Kung-Lu. And in the Congo there was another apelike animal called the Kakundakari.

Dr. Theodore Flagg was mentioned or quoted in almost every article. In one of the articles, he said that since 1990 seven totally new species of monkey had been found in South America alone. He maintained that if these primates could remain hidden from scientists for so long, then it is highly likely that creatures closer to man, and therefore more intelligent, may yet be undiscovered. But there was no concrete proof that any of these giant primates actually existed. It was more along the lines of plaster proof in the form of footprint castings: the best evidence that the legend was true. Hundreds of footprints had been preserved over the years by pouring plaster of paris into the indentations left by the giant primate's footprints. Some of the castings were proven to be fake, but there were others that appeared to be real and scientists had no explanation for them. The footprints were up to twenty-two inches long and seven inches wide.

Encounters with the Sasquatch in the Pacific Northwest had been going on for a couple hundred years. One of the oldest descriptions was written by Spanish naturalist Jose Mozino while he was exploring British Columbia in 1792. He wrote of an animal called the Matlox,

. . . an inhabitant of the mountainous country, of who all have an unspeakable terror. They figure it has a monstrous body, all covered with black animal hair; the head like a human; but the eye teeth very sharp and strong, like those of a bear; the arms very large, and the toes and fingers armed with large curved nails. His howl falls to the ground those who hear him, and he smashes into a thousand pieces the unfortunate on whom a blow his hand falls.

Native Americans had a number of different names for the Sasquatch. The Huppa of Northern California called it Oh-mah-'ah. The Skagit people believed in Kala'litabiqw (don't worry, I can't pronounce this either), an animal that had moss growing on his head who could cross the Cascade mountains in a single stride. Other Northwest tribes kept their children close to home with tales of the Steta'l, a race of mountain giants that stole children. The name Bigfoot was given to the animal in 1958 when a newspaper ran a photo of a huge footprint supposedly belonging to a Sasquatch.

There was a film of Bigfoot shot in 1967 in northern California. I found a couple frames of the film on a website. It looked like a human in a gorilla suit to me. The photos Clyde Smithers had shown were a lot more convincing than the frames from the film, but even Clyde's photos could have been faked. Newspapers and television shows would pay a bundle for a genuine photo of a Sasquatch.

A number of people claimed to have seen a Sasquatch. Dozens of these sightings had taken place in the Pacific Northwest with many occurring around Mount Saint Helens. Enough people had seen Sasquatch over the years to come up with a portrait or profile: the Sasquatch walks on two legs and is six to eleven feet tall, weighing between 700 and 2,500 pounds. The difference in size was attributed to the existence of young Sasquatch. He (or she) is often described as apelike with a broad, flattened nose and a slitlike, lipless mouth. It has a sloping forehead that is covered by bangs or a fringe of hair said to be five to seven inches long. Its eyes are thought to reflect light, which is usually associated with nocturnal behavior. The skin color is said to be dark and hair color is usually reported as auburn or black, but on occasion beige, white, and silver. The Sasquatch are said to be shy, but will act aggressively when threatened or injured. They do not speak, but are said to emit a roaring scream like no other animal on earth. Those who have been near a Sasquatch say that it has a terrible odor, like that of rotting meat. No one knows how long a Sasquatch lives.

Some of the Sasquatch encounters I read about were pretty wild. One guy even claimed that a Sasquatch had picked him up in his sleeping bag while he was asleep and carried him to its camp where he was held prisoner for several days. This particular Sasquatch had a wife and kid. A lot of these stories seemed to be in the same category as close encounters with extraterrestrials. It was hard to believe that the stories were actually true.

Dad must have been the victim of a hoax. Maybe his buddies had lured him to Mount Saint Helens so they could play a trick on him.

About 2 A.M. I turned the computer off and decided to run my hoax theory by Dad before I went to sleep. He was sitting in his recliner reading a book.

"You're up late," he said.

"Yeah." Like I would be asleep with all this going on. "I was wondering about something."

Dad put the book down on his lap. "Go ahead."

"Are you sure your friends didn't play a trick on you?"

"What do you mean?"

"Well, let's say they invite you out hunting and one of them puts on a gorilla suit and jumps out at you. They don't expect you to fall down the hill and hurt yourself. To cover themselves they build a shelter and put you in it."

"Why wouldn't they just tell me what they did?"

"Because you might get mad and fire them."

He thought about it for a minute. "It's not a bad theory, but there's a little problem with it. What are the chances of Clyde Smithers getting photos of Sasquatch on the exact same hillside three and a half months later?"

I had to admit that it was quite a coincidence. "How do you know it's the same hill, or the same mountain for that matter? Clyde didn't say where he took the photos. He could have been on Mount Hood, or Mount Adams, or . . . "

"Believe me, I know, Dylan."

"Maybe you built the shelter yourself," I suggested. "You stumbled away from the hillside and in your stupor, built the shelter, then forgot you did it."

Dad shook his head. "I know this is all hard to believe, Dylan. Until I saw Clyde's photos, I wasn't sure I believed it myself."

"Did you go back to the slope and look?"

"No," he said quietly and looked away. "I was too afraid."

CHAPTER 3

I WENT BACK UP to my room. Could there really be a gigantic primate running around Mount Saint Helens that no one knows about? If the Sasquatch doesn't exist, what had Dad and the others seen? Dad is a little on the crazy side, but I don't think he would make something like this up. He had seen something, or he believed he saw something, and those photos at the B.F.I. meeting looked real to me. Thoughts like these kept me up until four o'clock in the morning.

The next day at school I floated through my classes like I was in a dream. At swim practice I somehow managed to do my laps without drowning.

By the time I got home I was like a zombie. Dad wasn't there. I stumbled into the kitchen to rummage around for something to eat and saw a newspaper on the counter. Dad must have bought it to see what they had said about the B.F.I. meeting.

Very little as it turned out. The only mention it got was

a small item in Section D with a photograph of Clyde Smithers at the pulpit. The headline read: LOCAL MAN CLAIMS BIGFOOT PHOTO. The article went on to debunk the whole Sasquatch phenomenon, stopping just short of calling Clyde an outright liar. I heard a car pull into the driveway and a moment later Dad came into the kitchen.

"No photo," he said, "no front page. I suspect they buried the story to punish Clyde for trying to sell them the photos. It's just as well."

"Where have you been?" I asked.

"Shopping. I need a hand with the groceries."

I was sure happy to hear this. It not only meant that we would have food in the house, it also meant that Dad might be getting back to normal.

I was wrong. Dad had gone grocery shopping all right. He had also bought a brand-new four-wheel-drive pickup truck to carry the groceries in. It was red and had a winch bolted to the front bumper that was big enough to pull the house down. He walked around back and opened the tailgate.

"Why did you get this?" I asked.

"I never liked your mom's Bug," he said. "Too small, too dangerous. As I was driving it to the mechanic I saw this beauty and traded it in."

Mom was going to kill him when she got back from Egypt. She loved her little Bug.

"I don't think she's going to like it," I said.

"What do you mean? Red is her favorite color." He put a grocery bag in my arms and I followed him into the kitchen.

"Seriously," I said, "why did you get the truck?"

He opened the cupboard and began putting boxes of cereal on the shelf. "Because I'm going back up there."

"When?"

"I'm not sure, but soon."

"Why?"

"I don't know. I just have to go back there."

"You know, Dad, this is really nuts."

"I know it must seem that way, Dylan. But what am I going to do? Pretend I didn't see what I saw?"

I tried to think of what Mom would say to talk him out of this.

"Then I'm going with you," I said.

"I don't think so, Dylan. It could be dangerous. Besides, you don't even believe in the Sasquatch."

"You mean the Matlox," I said. "Also known as Oh-mah-'ah, or Steta'l, or . . ."

He grinned. "You've been tinkering. Where did you pick up that stuff?"

"On the Internet. So, how about it?"

"You have school."

"Spring vacation is coming up," I said. "I'm not

about to let you do this alone. I'd worry the whole time you're up there. You can't do that to me."

This was a pretty fair imitation of Mom and I could see her logic working its magic on him. He was trying to think of something to say that would put an end to my idea, but nothing was squeezing through.

"Fine," he said. "We'll do it together."

"Great."

I figured that we would spend a few days on Mount Saint Helens, see nothing, and that would be the end of it. He would start tinkering with something else.

After we ate I went upstairs to do my homework, but as soon as I saw the bed I changed my mind. The next thing I knew Dad was shaking me awake. The room was dark.

"What time is it?"

"About 9:30, partner. And we have a meeting."

I sat up. "Meeting?"

"Dr. Flagg has finally arrived. The cryptozoologist. He's giving a presentation at the church."

"Kind of late for a meeting, isn't it?" All I wanted to do was go back to sleep. I considered asking him if he wouldn't mind going alone, but instead, I swung my feet out of bed. If I didn't go with him he might assume I wasn't interested and pursue the Sasquatch on his own. With Dad you were either in or you were out.

"I saw Dr. Flagg's name on several Web pages."

"I'm not surprised. He's the world's leading authority on cryptids. He represents the militant wing of cryptid researchers."

"What do you mean by militant?"

"I'll tell you on the way. We've got to get going."

Dad explained that there were four basic approaches to solving the Sasquatch mystery. One group of people were trying to capture a Sasquatch alive. Their plan was to shoot one with a tranquilizer dart, or trap it somehow, and bring it into captivity to study. Another group wanted to get close enough to a Sasquatch and use a thing called a K-dart on it. The dart takes out a chunk of flesh without causing permanent damage to the animal. By analyzing the DNA from the dart, scientists would be able to determine if the Sasquatch was a new species. The third group, headed by Dr. Flagg, believed that the only way to prove that the Sasquatch really existed was to bring one in—dead or alive.

"That seems a little severe," I said.

"Perhaps," Dad said. "But all three approaches are legitimate. Ultimately, they all want to protect the Sasquatch, but legal protection can't happen until the animal is proven to exist. There are a lot of political considerations. If it was proven beyond a doubt that the Sasquatch existed here, it could virtually shut down logging in the Pacific

Northwest. A few years ago concern for the endangered spotted owl shut down logging in some areas. You can imagine what would happen if we discovered a brand-new species of primate living in the woods. It would take years to sort it all out, and in the meantime thousands of timber workers would lose their jobs."

"So, loggers aren't exactly thrilled at the prospect of Sasquatch existing."

Dad laughed. "That's putting it mildly. Some people believe the forestry industry is behind some of the Sasquatch hoaxes. The best way to discredit something is to prove that it's a hoax. They claim that foresters hire people to go out into the woods and lay fake footprints, doctor photographs . . ."

"And put on gorilla suits," I added.

Dad sighed and shook his head. "That too, Dylan. I don't expect you to believe me. You weren't there, but it wasn't a gorilla suit."

"You said there were four approaches to the Sasquatch problem," I said, changing the subject.

"The fourth group believes we should just leave the Sasquatch alone."

"Which group are you with?"

"At this point, none of the above," he said. "I need to learn more. That's why I want to hear what Dr. Flagg has to say."

Dad had a little trouble parallel parking the huge truck outside the church. I wondered how he was going to handle the red tank when he took it off-road. I guess I would find out. Someone was standing at the door of the church and asked for Dad's B.F.I. membership card.

"I thought this was an open meeting," Dad said.

"Dr. Flagg has requested that only long-term members be admitted."

"Since when was he elected president of this chapter?"

The man answered with a helpless shrug. Dad got his wallet out and showed his membership card.

"You've only been a member for four months," the man said. "I'll have to get someone to vouch for you. Do you know any members?"

"Joe West and Clyde Smithers," Dad said impatiently.

"Hang on." He sent another man off to look for them. A minute later the man returned and nodded. "I guess you're okay. Sorry about the hassle. Dr. Flagg is trying to make sure the press doesn't get in. You know how it is."

We squeezed by him. There was plenty of room inside. We sat on a pew about midway down the aisle. Up front there was a long table. Sitting at it were Joe West, Clyde Smithers, and a couple other people I recognized from the night before. Clyde didn't look very happy. Sitting next to him was an older man who looked like he had just been on a shopping spree at Abercrombie & Fitch. Everything he wore was made out of khaki material, including his vest, which had about a hundred pockets on it. He wore a heavy gold chain around his neck, his long gray hair was combed straight back, and he had a short, carefully clipped gray beard. This had to be the famous cryptozoologist Dr. Theodore Flagg.

Joe West walked up to the pulpit. "It looks like we'll have a much calmer meeting tonight," he began. "The board has spent most of the day talking about Clyde's photos and figuring out what we should do about this new evidence."

"Arguing is more like it," Clyde grumbled.

"That too," Joe continued. He looked more at ease tonight and he wasn't sweating. "For those who don't know him, this is Dr. Theodore Flagg and he has a few things to say. We won't keep you very long this evening. Dr. Flagg?"

Dr. Flagg stood up. He was shorter than I expected—maybe five feet seven inches or so. And now that he was standing, I could see that his clothes were somewhat ragged and soiled as if he hadn't changed them in a while. He walked over to the pulpit and pulled the microphone down to his mouth, which was about a foot lower than Joe's. He looked out at the small crowd for a few seconds without saying anything to make sure he had our attention, then he began.

"First, I want to say that I was glad my airplane was delayed last night." He had a deep theatrical voice with a slight British accent. "It sounded rather like a three-ring-circus here."

A few people in the audience laughed.

"You were lucky that the local newspaper buried its coverage. Publicity is the worst thing that could happen right now. I can understand Clyde's desire to show his remarkable photographs." He glanced at Clyde. "But they need to be authenticated before they are released . . ."

"You mean sold," Clyde said.

Dr. Flagg nodded. "Clyde has agreed not to publish or show the photos until I can have them verified. I believe they are real, but there are a number of people out there who will disagree with me. I don't want to give them any ammunition. Clyde has also agreed to show us where he took the photographs."

It was Clyde's turn to nod, but he didn't do it very enthusiastically.

"For showing us, Clyde will become a full member of the team."

"But my brothers still have to pay and that's twenty thousand bucks!" Clyde said bitterly, glaring at Dr.

Flagg who totally ignored the comment.

"What team?" someone from the audience asked.

"We are forming an expedition to track down this cryptid."

"And kill it?"

"We might as well get right to it," Dr. Flagg said gravely. "Yes, we are going after the cryptid aggressively."

There was a lot of shouting all at once. Several people in the audience were very upset by the news. Dr. Flagg calmly stood at the pulpit without saying a word and let people shout as if he had seen this kind of reaction many times before. I looked at Dad and couldn't tell if he was upset or not. He simply stared straight ahead. After awhile the shouting died down.

"May I continue?" Dr. Flagg asked quietly. "I assume that most of you are here because you believe the Sasquatch is real. I have spent most of my adult life trying to prove this. Despite the photographs, footprints, eyewitness reports, and hair samples, the scientific community thinks the Sasquatch is nothing more than a persistent myth. The only thing that is going to change their minds is to see the animal with their own eyes."

"What do you propose to do?" a woman in the front row asked.

"We are setting up a limited partnership," he said. "It's the only way to deal with all the publicity, and quite frankly, the money that will result from bringing a Sasquatch in. We are selling shares for ten thousand dollars to raise money for the expedition. This offer will be effective for one week. After we bring in the Sasquatch any and all profits will be divided equally among the partners."

"Can you buy more than one share?"

"Yes."

"Who's going on this expedition?"

"That has not been decided yet. The only thing I know is that we are going to keep it small, and relatively quiet. We don't want any publicity at this point. That will only bring people out into the woods with their four-wheel-drive vehicles and rifles."

I thought of the red truck and looked at Dad.

"Do you have to go on the expedition to become a full partner?"

"No. In fact, we already have several investors who have put up money and they have no interest in accompanying us. If we are successful, they will share equally in any profits.

"I have already hired a professional tracker. He will be arriving in the next few days. He will be paid for his services and will not get a percentage of the profits."

"Who is he?"

"I'd rather not say at this point."

"What type of profits do you expect from this venture?"

"That's difficult to say, but the film and book rights alone should be considerable. To say nothing of the . . ."

"Why don't you just leave the Sasquatch alone?" a voice behind us asked.

Dad and I turned around. An old man was on his feet glaring at Dr. Flagg.

"Because the Sasquatch cannot be protected until it is proven to exist," Dr. Flagg said, smoothly.

"What if you fools go out there and get lucky and shoot the last one."

"I doubt that this Sasquatch is the last one," Dr. Flagg said.

"I know that man," Dad whispered. "But I can't place him."

"When Mount Saint Helens erupted in 1980," Dr. Flagg said, "I thought it might have killed all the Sasquatch in the area. But Clyde's photos have proven me wrong. And if there is only one Sasquatch left, what difference does it make? He or she can't reproduce on its own. That would be a first for a primate."

More laughter.

"If there is only one left we might as well get a good look at it before it disappears forever. But I want to emphasize that I don't believe this is the last Sasquatch on earth or even in the Northwest. The chances of that are very, very slim. If we bring a Sasquatch in, animals like it all over the world will be protected."

"Well, I think it's wrong," the old man said. "Very wrong. You're talking about murder here . . ."

"Sir, I don't want to get in a debate about this with you. I can promise you that I have not made this decision lightly. If there was another way I would certainly follow that course. I'm trying to protect the species, not destroy it. If this Sasquatch was capable of knowing what's at stake, I'm sure it would gladly sacrifice itself to save all of its kind."

"What a crock! The Sasquatch would have revealed themselves a long time ago if it was as simple as that. I think they just want to be left alone."

"That may be," Dr. Flagg said, shaking his head sadly. "But they are not alone. They live in a world crowded with human beings and it is getting more crowded everyday. The only way to protect the Sasquatch is to prove they exist. I wish there was another way, but I'm afraid there isn't."

"You're a fool, Dr. Flagg, and so is anyone else that agrees with you." He made eye contact with everyone at the front table, then sat down.

Dr. Flagg looked around the small crowd, but no one appeared to have any more questions or comments. "If you are interested in becoming a partner come up to the front. One week from tonight we will stop accepting investors. In the meantime, I'll be working out the logistics of this expedition."

Dr. Flagg left the pulpit and joined the others at the table.

Joe stood up. "I guess that's it folks. We're going to be kind of busy during the next few weeks, so we won't be having meetings for awhile. Hopefully, the next time we get together we'll have some big news. If any of you decide to join us during the next week, you know how to get in touch with me. Thanks for coming tonight."

Dad stood up, and for a second I thought he was going to rush up to the front. Instead, he turned around and looked for the old man who had spoken, but he must have slipped out while our backs were turned because he was nowhere to be seen.

CHAPTER 4

WHEN I GOT OUT of school the next afternoon, Dad was waiting for me at the curb in the red truck. Doug Groves and a couple other friends were talking to him through the window. He hadn't told me he was going to pick me up and I hoped he wasn't telling them why he had gotten the truck. They already knew he was a little strange, but they didn't need to know that he believed in giant cryptids. I worked my way through my friends to the passenger door. None of them were laughing or looking like they felt sorry for me, so I figured Dad had kept his mouth shut about the Sasquatch.

As soon as we pulled away from the curb he said excitedly, "I know who that old man is."

"What old man?"

"From the B.F.I. meeting."

The man who didn't like Dr. Flagg. I had almost forgotten about him. In fact I was trying very hard to forget this whole Sasquatch thing in the hope that it would all go away. To keep my mind off hairy giants I had concentrated on my schoolwork. Mom wanted me to send my report card to her in Egypt and I wanted it to be halfway decent so she wouldn't worry.

"He's one of my renters!"

"You didn't recognize him last night?"

"I haven't seen him in ten years. He lives in one of the houses I have down on Cedar Street. Actually, he was living in the house when I bought it, and stayed on as a renter. He sends his rent to the office every month and never calls me about anything. A perfect tenant. All I do is drive by a couple times a year and make sure the house is still there. His name is Buckley Johnson."

"And we're going to pay him a visit?"

"Right."

"Did you join the expedition?"

When we got home from the meeting the night before he hadn't made up his mind yet. He said that he was impressed with Dr. Flagg, but he wasn't going to jump into anything.

"I have six more days," he said.

We turned onto Cedar, which is only a couple miles from our house. The street was lined with neat little houses with well-manicured yards.

"How many houses do you own here?"

"Six," he said. "Would you look at that?" He stopped the truck. To our right was a house whose yard hadn't been cut in several months. Old, soggy newspapers were piled up on the front porch and the screen door was dangling by one hinge.

"Is that Mr. Johnson's house?"

"No, he lives right across the street."

Mr. Johnson's house had a white picket fence, a perfect little yard, and a swinging chair on the porch.

"Then who lives in that dump?" I asked.

"I don't know. The office rented it out. I bought it a couple of years ago and fixed it up. It was in perfect shape. Maybe my renters moved out and the office doesn't know or forgot to tell me. We manage so many rentals that they sometimes slip through the cracks. But first thing's first." He pulled into Mr. Johnson's driveway.

"What are you going to say to him?"

"I'm going to ask him what he knows about the Sasquatch." Dad believed in getting right to the point.

We walked up to the front door and rang the bell. No one answered.

"Let's see if he's around back."

Dad walked down the narrow driveway a few feet ahead of me. When he turned the corner into the backyard he shouted and stumbled back into the driveway. I ran up to him.

"What happened? What's the matter?"

He was gasping for breath and couldn't speak. I thought he was having a heart attack.

"There," he managed to say and pointed.

I turned around and jumped backward. Standing next to the house was a Sasquatch! The top of its head was even with Mr. Johnson's rain gutters. I was surprised Dad *didn't* have a heart attack! I almost had one myself when I saw it. Of course, it wasn't real. Sasquatch don't hang out in neighborhoods. But it sure looked real from what little I knew. Mr. Johnson had carved a life-size replica of the beast.

"Wow," Dad said, having regained his breath and part of his composure. "I didn't expect to see that!"

We looked at each other and started laughing. It had been a long time since we had done that, and it felt good.

I realized this was exactly what happened to Dad on Mount Saint Helens. He climbed to the top of the hill, saw the Sasquatch, then stumbled backward. Clyde Smither's photo didn't give me a sense of how big Sasquatch were. It looked like it was three times the size of the gorillas I had seen at the zoo. I now had some idea why Dad was so haunted by the event. I couldn't imagine what it would be like to see a real Sasquatch.

"How could something this big stay hidden from humans for hundreds of years?"

"Not all humans," Dad said. "Just the ones that count." He walked up to the giant carving for a closer look. The top of his head was just above the Sasquatch's waist.

"If this is Mr. Johnson's work, he's a pretty good artist," Dad said. "The color is off. The one I saw wasn't this dark, but the size and shape are right on and the face is perfect."

The Sasquatch was looking down at Dad through half-closed eyes. It had a slight grin as if it were mildly amused at what it saw.

I glanced around the backyard. The Sasquatch wasn't alone. Over in the corner was a carved deer and two fawns. Across from them were a mother black bear and two cubs. The cubs were climbing the trunk of a large cedar.

"There's a Polaroid camera in the truck," Dad said. "I want to get a picture of this."

I ran off to get the camera. When I got back Dad was scribbling on the back of one of his business cards.

"Mr. Johnson isn't home," he said as he gave me the card. "Slip this into the mail slot in his front door. I'll take a photo of our friend and we'll go across the street and see what's going on there."

We left the truck in Mr. Johnson's driveway and

walked across the street to the other rental. Dad banged on the front door, but no one answered. The backyard was as wild as Mr. Johnson's was well-kept. Dad knocked on the back door, then opened the screen and turned the knob. The door opened.

"Maybe we should just leave a card," I suggested.

"Relax," Dad said. "We're not trespassing. I own this house." He stepped inside. "Anybody home? I'm the owner, Mr. Hickock, and we're coming inside."

In the kitchen there were at least a dozen large pizza boxes stacked neatly on the counter. Next to them was a coffee maker with the pot half-full and the light still on. I thought Dad would leave when he realized that someone was actually living in the house, but he didn't. He opened the refrigerator. The only thing inside were two large bottles of Pepsi.

"Anybody home?" He pushed open the door leading to the living room. "What do we have here?"

There was a cot, a recliner, a small color television, a 35-mm camera on a tripod with a long lens facing the front window, a video camera on a tripod facing the same window, and an expensive looking reel-to-reel tape recorder with headphones. Other than this equipment there wasn't any other furniture.

"Interesting decor," Dad said. "Late American Spy Master."

"What is all this?" I asked.

"If I had to bet, I would say that this is a stakeout house." He looked through the camera. "Take a look at this."

I looked through the viewfinder. The lens was centered right in the middle of Mr. Johnson's front door.

"Why would someone be watching Mr. Johnson?" I asked.

Dad took a scrap of paper out of his pocket and got out his cell phone. He dialed a number; the reel-to-reel clicked on and the tape started moving. He hung up and the tape stopped.

"Whoever they are, they've also tapped Mr. Johnson's phone."

"Police?"

"I don't know." He took a Polaroid photo of the setup and stuck it in his pocket. "Let's go to the real estate office and see what we can find out."

By the time we got there everyone had left for the day.

"Do you know how to turn this on?" Dad asked, pointing to the computer.

"You know, Dad, you should really learn how to use a computer. I think they're here to stay. Like I told you, I found a lot of information about the Sasquatch on the Web."

"On the what?"

He was hopeless. I turned the computer on. When the screen lit up it asked for a password.

"Hickock," Dad said.

"That's original." I typed in our last name, pushed the "rentals" prompt, then scrolled down the screen until I found the Cedar Street properties.

"This one." Dad pointed at an address.

I highlighted it and opened the file.

The man who had rented the house across from Mr. Johnson was named Peter Nunn. He had been in the house for eighteen months. I scrolled through the rest of the information, but there wasn't much besides the fact that Mr. Nunn paid his rent on time.

"So, what do you think is going on?"

Dad shook his head. "Bring up Mr. Johnson's record."

I typed in his name. There was a little more information about Mr. Johnson, but nothing that would help us. When Dad bought the property Mr. Johnson was working for the Fish and Wildlife Service.

"Now I remember," he said. "He was some kind of biologist or something. At the time I think he had been with the service for over twenty years. This information is ten years old. Mr. Johnson is probably retired by now. I think his wife died a long time ago."

Dad's cell phone rang.

"Hello? . . . Thanks for calling back, Mr. Johnson. I'd like to get together with you and talk about the meeting last night . . . That would be great. We'll be there at seven." He flipped the phone closed. "We're meeting Mr. Johnson at Teter's restaurant for dinner."

We got to the restaurant a few minutes before seven. I was famished and wanted to order as soon as we sat down, but Dad said that we had to wait for Mr. Johnson. By seven-thirty I was about ready to pass out from hunger.

"Maybe he got arrested," I said.

"And maybe the people watching him aren't the police."

"Who else would be watching him?"

Dad shrugged his shoulders. "I don't know, but I don't want you asking him about it. What's going on in his personal life isn't our concern."

I was about ready to disagree with him when I saw Mr. Johnson limp through the front door. He was using an unusual-looking walking stick to steady himself. It was at least four feet long and made out of some kind of knotty wood. Dad stood up and waved. Everyone in the restaurant turned to look at Mr. Johnson as he made his way over to our table.

"Thanks for coming, Mr. Johnson," Dad said and

gave him what Mom and I called his "realty" smile.

Mr. Johnson didn't seem impressed with the smile and didn't apologize for being forty-five minutes late. He stared down at me. "Who's this?"

"This is my son, Dylan."

"Well, scoot over, Dylan, so I can sit down." I moved over and he set the stick between us. Now that it was closer I saw that the knots were actually miniature carvings. The head near the top of the staff was a Sasquatch. When Mr. Johnson saw me looking at it, he moved it to his other side.

Mr. Johnson was in pretty good shape for an old guy. He was thin, but looked strong. If it weren't for his limp, I would have guessed that he was a long-distance runner. He had a full head of white hair and light brown eyes that darted around the restaurant like a hawk's looking for a mouse. From my side of the table he could see everyone coming into the restaurant, which was probably why he sat down next to me. By the way he was checking out every new customer that walked through the door, I suspected he knew he was being watched.

"What can I do for you, Hickock?"

"I wanted to talk to you about the Sasquatch."

"I saw you at the meeting last night," he said. "What about them?"

"We were just about ready to order some food," Dad

said. "Would you like something?" I guess he didn't want to discuss cryptids on an empty stomach and neither did I.

"I already ate."

"I hope you don't mind if we eat. If I don't get some food into Dylan soon we might have a medical emergency on our hands."

"A young boy can't run on an empty tank," Mr. Johnson said. "I'll just take a cup of tea."

I ordered the biggest hamburger on the menu, a milk shake, a plate of fries, and a slice of apple pie with vanilla ice cream.

"So, what do you want to know?" Mr. Johnson asked after the waiter walked away with our orders.

"I'm a little new to all this," Dad started out. "You seemed to have a strong objection to Dr. Flagg's plan. I want to hear more about why."

"Two reasons. One, I'm opposed to murder. Two, Flagg is a glory-seeking fool. He's obsessed with Sasquatch."

I thought about the life-sized sculpture in his backyard and wondered who was obsessed. "If you don't believe me you should have seen him this afternoon at the meeting."

"Meeting?"

"Private planning meeting for the so-called shareholders. That's where I was when you came by. I showed up at Joe West's to give him my ten thousand dollars, and they were all there, crowded into that little shack he has in back of his place. They looked like a bunch of kids in a club house up to no good. Joe's wife doesn't believe in the Sasquatch and won't let anyone in the house that does, except for Joe from time to time."

"I'm surprised that you would want to join them after what you said last night."

"You're not the only one," Mr. Johnson said with a laugh. "I shouldn't have opened my big mouth at the meeting. Probably won't be the last time. I thought I would get more support, but everyone sat there, like God was talking to them from that pulpit."

"What happened at the meeting this afternoon?"

"Well, they didn't take my money if that's what you're asking. I got blackballed. They didn't want me in their club. Boo-hoo."

"Do you know what they're planning?"

"They are going to hunt down a Sasquatch and kill it. If they succeed they are going to make a lot of money and become famous. If they fail, Flagg isn't out a dime because he's not putting any dough in the pot. In fact, he's going to be paid a bucket of money as the expedition's technical adviser. I was hoping that the whole thing was a scam—a way for Flagg to make some fast cash and get a wheelbarrow full of publicity for himself, but it looks like he's really going to go after the Sasquatch this time."

"Dr. Flagg didn't seem interested in publicity," my dad said.

Mr. Johnson laughed, "What a joke. The only reason he didn't like the publicity over Clyde's photos was because it didn't center around the fabulous Dr. Flagg. He wants to keep it quiet at this point so he can get more glory later. Just wait and see."

The food arrived and I started wolfing it down.

"I guess I don't understand," Dad said. "If you're against their plan why did you try to give them ten thousand dollars?"

"I figured that joining them was the best way to keep track of what they were doing."

"What are you going to do now?"

"That remains to be seen. But enough about me. What's your interest in this whole thing?"

Dad looked down at his food for a few seconds. I was halfway through mine, but he hadn't touched his yet. When he looked up he said, "I saw a Sasquatch . . ." He told Mr. Johnson the entire story.

Mr. Johnson didn't blink or change his expression during Dad's strange tale. When he finished, Mr. Johnson continued to stare at him. "Did you know anything about the Sasquatch before this happened?" he asked.

"Very little."

"I'm curious about that shelter. How was it made?"

"The bed was made out of a pile of small fir boughs. The top was made out of large branches leaning against the trunk of a tree. When I regained consciousness, the first thing I smelled was pitch, so the shelter was freshly made. The branches weren't cut with an ax; they looked like they had been broken off, and some of them were a pretty good size."

"Did you see any footprints?"

"No, but I wasn't really looking. When I came to I was disoriented and confused."

"Understandable. And who have you told about this?"

"You, Dylan, and some of the people at B.F.I."

"Clyde Smithers?"

Dad nodded. "I also told him where I had seen the Sasquatch."

"So, that's how he found the spot."

"I assume so."

"Old Clyde doesn't have a job. He spends most of his time wandering around the woods with his look-alike brothers, as if one Clyde isn't enough. They say he hasn't been quite right in the head since he got kidnapped by those aliens a few years back."

"Aliens?"

"So he claims. They took him up into their space-ship and transported him to a planet called Zona where he married some kind of princess. He had a falling-out with her and the king about how their child was going to be raised so they sent him back to Earth."

Mr. Johnson grinned at our shocked expressions. "You know his two brothers are deaf mutes?"

Dad nodded. He hadn't told me about that.

"The rumor is that Clyde was an only child. The brothers are actually clones given to Clyde as a wedding present when he was on Zona. Apparently they don't have vocal chords up there, which is why Clyde's clones can't talk. Clyde is about as loony as they come, but I trust him a lot more than I trust Flagg."

"What's the connection between aliens and his interest in Sasquatch?" Dad asked.

"Clyde claims there's a gate to Zona on Mount Saint Helens and the Sasquatch are the guardians of the gate. He wants to go back up to Zona and bring his son down to Earth. Pretty bizarre, huh?"

Dad didn't seem bothered by this story, which worried me quite a bit.

"Do you think you would be able to find this hill again?" Mr. Johnson asked.

"I know exactly where it is."

"Where?"

"I don't think I should say. I already made that mistake once and now look what's happened."

"I was just curious." Mr. Johnson picked up his stick and looked at it for a moment. "My advice, Hickock, is for you to forget this whole thing. Just let it go and get on with your life."

"That's good advice," I said.

Dad looked at me. "I'm not sure I can do that."

Mr. Johnson nodded and stood up. "I don't know what you saw, Hickock. Or if you saw anything. But I do know that Flagg is going to try to find and kill a Sasquatch. If I were you I would think twice about helping him murder an animal that built a shelter for you and put you in it."

"I appreciate your time, Mr. Johnson."

"Please call me Buck." He looked at me. "Both of you."

"One more thing," Dad said. "Why are you interested in the Sasquatch? We saw the sculpture in the backyard. It looked just like the animal I saw. It scared me half to death."

"Startling, isn't it? Keeps the neighbor kids out of the yard and the crows out of my garden."

"So you've seen a Sasquatch."

"In my dreams, Hickock," Mr. Johnson said. "In my

dreams." He limped out of the restaurant leaning on his stick.

We stayed at the restaurant long enough for me to finish Dad's food.

On the way home we drove by Mr. Johnson's house. A light was on inside. The house across the street was dark, but there was a green Ford Taurus in the driveway.

PART TWO

THE MOUNTAIN

He looks at the earth
and it trembles,
He touches the mountains
and they smoke.

—Psalm 104:32

CHAPTER 5

"WHAT'S GOING ON, Dylan? Ever since your mom left for Egypt you've been acting pretty weird," Doug said.

We were standing outside Mr. Rhodes's classroom where we had just watched a video about the 1980 eruption of Mount Saint Helens. The blast was heard 300 miles away, but the sound moved upward with such velocity that the people on the mountain that day didn't hear the explosion. They said the eruption was like detonating the Hiroshima bomb every second for seven and a half hours. The 60,000-foot ash plume was so violent there were lightning storms inside it.

When the bell rang I had wandered out of class in a daze wondering if the Sasquatch knew the mountain was going to erupt beforehand. When they felt the earthquakes in the months leading up to the eruption, did they leave the area? Or did some of them stay on the mountain like the loggers, tourists, and residents who were never seen again? I kept going back and forth between believing in the Sasquatch and thinking the whole thing was some kind of hallucination. After Mr. Johnson told us about Clyde's abduction to the planet Zona, I started doubting again. But by morning I had slid back into half-belief. Dad had seen something. And Mr. Johnson seemed to believe, and he didn't strike me as a fool.

"Dylan?" Doug said.

"Yeah?"

"Did you hear what I said?"

"Sorry, I guess I blanked out."

"You've been blanking out for days! You haven't answered the E-mail I've sent you, you haven't been over to the house. What have you been doing?"

"Helping my dad with some things."

"So that's it. What's the madman up to now?"

"Oh, it's nothing like that," I lied. Doug knew all about Dad's tinkering, but I wasn't about to tell him about this Sasquatch thing. "I'm helping him with some of his rental properties. He has a lot of vacancies and he's getting them ready to rent out."

"His new truck is awesome. Does your mom know about it?" he asked with an evil grin. Doug knew my mom pretty well, too—at least well enough to know that she was going to blow a gasket when she saw the red truck.

"Not yet."

Doug shook his head. "When she gets back, she'll probably run him over with it. Have you heard from her?"

"She phoned when she got to Cairo, but I wasn't there when she called." And it was just as well. I don't know if I could have stopped myself from spilling my guts about Sasquatch.

"So, what are you doing for spring vacation?"

"Just hanging around. Helping my dad."

"Boy, that sure sounds like a lot of fun."

The bell rang and Doug ran off to his next class. I was happy to see him go so I wouldn't have to make up more lies. Dad and I were going to spend spring vacation on Mount Saint Helens. I wasn't thrilled about the idea. First, we had never even camped out in the backyard together. Second, the mountain could erupt again any day. That's why Mr. Rhodes had shown us the video. I was going to try to get a copy at the library and show it to Dad. Maybe the possibility of being buried under six hundred feet of pyroclastic mud flows would dampen his Sasquatch tinkering.

When school got out I half expected Dad to be waiting for me out front again, but he wasn't there. I started walking home before Doug or one of my other friends came out. I was getting pretty fed up with the whole situation and wished Dad had never seen the Sasquatch, or whatever he thought he saw. I just wanted my old boring life back. My only hope was that after we spent a week suffering on the mountain, Dad would forget the whole thing and get back to his normal insanity. Tinkering with the Titanic seemed pretty normal compared to this.

After our dinner with Mr. Johnson, Dad went into the garage and sat in his chair—for three days! This was the first time he had ever done anything like that. He didn't even get up to go to bed. He said he was working things out. Every time I checked on him he was just sitting there staring into space. He wasn't even reading a book. I figured that he was trying to let the Sasquatch idea go as Mr. Johnson suggested, and that he was having a hard time.

So, you can imagine my shock when I got home and found Dr. Flagg, Joe West, Clyde Smithers, the Clones, and a couple other guys in our living room. They were kneeling around a large map laid out on the floor.

Dr. Flagg was the first to notice me. "You must be Dylan," he said, standing up. He was shorter than I was and dressed in the same khaki uniform he had worn at the church, and it wasn't getting any cleaner.

Dad came out of the kitchen carrying a big bag of potato chips. Joe West took the bag from him without a word and tore it open.

"Hi, Dylan, how was school?" Dad asked casually.

"What?" He acted as if this group of Sasquatch hunters were at the house after school every day. No big deal.

"School?" he repeated.

"It was fine," I said. "What's all . . ."

"Let's go into the kitchen and I'll tell you what's happening here."

"I'll come with you," Dr. Flagg said.

I followed Dad into the kitchen with Dr. Flagg right behind me.

"Be cool," Dad whispered under his breath.

"What's that, Bill?" Dr. Flagg asked.

"I said it felt sort of cool in here," Dad answered. "I need to turn up the heat."

"Feels just fine to me," Dr. Flagg said.

"I joined the team this morning," Dad announced.

It took every ounce of control not to shout: *Have you completely lost your mind?* Be cool, I told myself and took a deep breath.

"Your father is a very important team member," Dr. Flagg said. He opened the refrigerator and pulled out a block of cheddar cheese. I watched in stunned silence as he opened several drawers until he found the one we kept the knives in. "We're roommates."

"Isn't that great?" Dad said before I could open my mouth.

Terrific, I thought and looked at my watch. It was 2 A.M. in Egypt. I could catch Mom at her hotel if she wasn't in the desert digging up mummies.

71

Dr. Flagg sat down at the table and sliced off a slab of cheese the size of a paperback book. "Your dad tells me that you are very interested in Sasquatch."

"Well, not exact—"

"Don't be modest, Dylan," Dad interrupted. "I told Dr. Flagg about all the Sasquatch research you've done on the Web."

I just stared at him. Before today he thought a web was something woven by a spider.

"I need to get back in with the others," Dr. Flagg said. "But before I do, I have a question for you, Dylan."

"Go ahead."

"Who have you told about the Sasquatch?"

"I didn't see a Sasquatch. I'm not even sure if I . . ."

"Dr. Flagg is talking about what we're doing. Who have you told about my seeing a Sasquatch and the plan to kill it?"

"Harvest, Bill," Dr. Flagg corrected. "Harvest."

Harvest? He was talking about the Sasquatch like it was a ripe peach. "No one," I said.

"Not even your friends at school?" Dr. Flagg asked.

I shook my head.

"That's heartening news!" Dr. Flagg exclaimed. "Your father said you could be trusted. You see, we really need to keep this quiet until we come back with a cryptid. You're going to be hearing a lot of things during the next few days that we can't afford to have publicized at this point. Can I count on you to keep this to yourself for the time being?"

I nodded.

"That's the spirit!" He walked out of the kitchen with his chunk of cheese.

"Dad, what is going on?"

"Outside," he whispered.

We walked out the backdoor and went into the garage, which looked like a staging area for a military invasion force. It was filled with sleeping bags, tents, radio equipment, rifles, boxes of cartridges, climbing gear, and other assorted gear.

"Where did all of this come from?" I asked.

"It's for the expedition."

"I can't believe you joined them!"

"It's the only way I can help the Sasquatch." He moved a stack of first-aid kits out of his chair and sat down.

"What do you mean?"

"Buck gave me the idea. I've spent the last three days thinking about what he said. If this animal tried to help me, the very least I can do is to try to help it. I had to join the team to keep track of what they are doing."

I wasn't happy about his decision, but I was glad to hear he wanted to help the Sasquatch, not kill one. "Why are they all at our house?"

"Buck was right about Joe's shack," he said. "It's a

73

miserable little place. Dr. Flagg wants the team to stay together until this thing is all over. He's afraid one of us will slip up and tell someone what we're planning to do, and the news media will get wind of the story. If the team lives in the same house, and watches each other, no one will be able to blab."

"Seems a little paranoid to me," I said.

Dad laughed. "You don't know the half of it. This secrecy thing is just a small part of Dr. Flagg's master plan. He's written a Sasquatch procedural manual outlining every step for bringing a Sasquatch in. It's over two hundred pages long! He's been waiting twenty years for the right moment and he thinks this is it. The manual covers every detail from how to get a 700 to 2,500-pound corpse out of the wilderness, to what to say to the newspeople when the team comes in with it."

I looked around the garage. "Well, they seem to be making themselves right at home," I said. "How are you going to stop them?"

"I have no idea. All I know is that I can't do it on my own. I want to get Buck involved somehow. Quietly."

"What can he do?"

"I don't know that either. I'm counting on you to find out."

"Me?"

Dad nodded. "The team agreed that no one will leave

the house alone, and we're not allowed to make private phone calls either. Flagg has disconnected all the phones except the cordless, and Joe's carrying that around. They even took my cell phone."

"Sounds like you've been grounded."

"But you're not. You have to go to school. Tomorrow afternoon I want you to go over to Buck's and tell him what we're doing."

"Aren't you forgetting something?"

"What?"

"The fact that Mr. Johnson is being watched."

"I don't know what that's all about. For all I know it's related to this Sasquatch thing. Which is why you'll need to get to his house without being seen. Just in case."

"What should I tell him?"

"Ask him if he'll stay near his phone for the next couple days. I'll try to give him a call when I can, but it might be late."

"And how do I get to Mr. Johnson's house in broad daylight without being seen?"

"There's an old alley that runs behind Cedar Street. It hasn't been used in years and it's overgrown. All you have to do is follow it until you get to his house, then climb over his fence and knock on the backdoor."

And now for the important question. "Am I going on the expedition with you?"

"I would feel a lot better if you stayed with Doug while I'm gone."

Meaning absolutely not. And I was about ready to howl in protest when Joe West walked into the garage clutching the half-empty bag of potato chips. The cordless phone was clipped to his belt. I wondered how Dad was going to get hold of it.

"What's happening?" Joe asked with a full mouth.

"Just showing Dylan the gear."

"Well, Dr. Flagg wants everyone inside."

"Sure, Joe. We'll be right along."

Joe reached into the bag, scooped out another paw full of chips, and stuffed them into his furry mouth. He waited for us to leave the garage, then followed us into the house.

CHAPTER 6

IT WAS MORE LIKE a jungle trail than an alley. In some places I had to crawl on my hands and knees through the brush. When I spotted the wooden Sasquatch, I climbed over the fence. Before I knocked on his backdoor I tried to clean some of the grime off my clothes without much success. Mr. Johnson opened the door and glared at me.

"Hello, Mr. Johnson. I'm Dylan Hickock, we had dinner a few nights . . . "

"I thought I told you to call me Buck."

"Sorry . . . Buck."

"Why did you come to the backdoor?"

"Uh . . ." I wasn't prepared for this question.

"And what have you been crawling around in?"

"Uh . . . I took a shortcut."

"Why did you come to the backdoor?" he asked again.

"Because your front door is being watched," I blurted out.

"How do you know that?"

I told him about going across the street during our first visit.

"What's inside there?"

"Video camera, still camera, tape recorder, and a lot of empty pizza boxes."

"Bad diet." He didn't seem at all surprised or upset that he was under surveillance. "So, what do you want?"

"My dad sent me. He needs your help."

"Well, maybe you should come inside then."

I stepped past him and walked through his small, tidy kitchen into the dining room, which had been converted into an office. I was surprised to see an elaborate computer set up on his desk. He must have been on the Web when I knocked on the backdoor because the page on the screen was still active. It was some kind of vitamin homepage. He switched he computer off before I got a good look at it.

"Let's go into the living room."

I followed him into the other room and sat down on the sofa. The blinds were closed and he had to turn on a couple of lights so we could see each other.

"I bet you're hungry," he said.

"Yeah, I guess I am."

"I have just the thing." He limped off toward the kitchen.

On the end table was a framed photograph of a pretty woman and a boy about my age. I wondered if they were Buck's family. Dad hadn't said anything about Buck having children. Across from me was an open door and I could just make out a weight set and a couple exercise machines. No wonder Buck was so fit.

He came back with a plate of sliced carrots. I hadn't seen carrots since Mom left for Egypt. She would like Buck.

"Thanks."

"Good roughage," he said. "Good for the eyes, too."

"I see you work out."

"I try," he said. "It hurts a little more these days. I guess my bones are getting brittle."

I was nervous and I didn't exactly know how to start. An old clock was ticking in another part of the house. A trickle of sweat ran down my left side.

I pointed at a photograph. "Is this your wife?"

"Betty. She's been dead a long time now."

"I'm sorry." I glanced at the closed blinds and thought it was a shame he couldn't keep them open. The room would have been a lot more cheerful with the sun lighting it up. "Why are they watching you?" This is not exactly how I intended to start out, but if Buck was bothered by the question, he didn't show it.

"It's not they, it's he. And it's not important."

"Peter Nunn," I said.

"Is that what he's calling himself?"

"That's not his name?"

Buck shook his head. "Didn't you say your dad needed help?"

"Yeah."

"Well, let's stick to that for now. What's going on?"

I told him everything I knew, which wasn't much. They were going to divide into three groups. Each team was going to search a section of the area where Clyde saw the Sasquatch.

"And who are on these teams?"

"Dad and Dr. Flagg are on one team and another guy who hasn't arrived yet. I think he's a professional tracker or something. The three Smithers are on the second team. And Joe West, Henry Polk, and Dean Voss make up the last team."

"So, you're not going with them?"

"I don't know." I hadn't had a chance to talk to Dad alone since the subject came up the night before. "Originally we were going to spend spring vacation up there, but things might have changed."

"Oh, things have changed all right. If I was your dad I wouldn't let you set foot on the mountain with that crowd."

Which is exactly why I thought I should go. Dad

would be up there all alone and there was no telling what he might try to do to help the Sasquatch.

"What are they going to do if they see a Sasquatch or come across some sign of one?" Buck asked.

"All I know is the teams will be in constant radio contact. If they spot a Sasquatch they'll try to surround it and kill it. Or 'harvest' it as Dr. Flagg put it."

Buck snorted in disgust. "Such a pretty word for murdering a totally innocent animal in cold blood. I don't know about your dad, but the others are pretty good woodsmen. There's a chance that they might just pull it off this time. I assume your dad wants to stop them."

"Or warn the Sasquatch or something. I don't think he really knows what he's going to do. That's why he wanted me to talk to you. He's going to give you a call when he can, but it might be late. Joe West is in charge of security. He doesn't let anybody out of his sight for more than about five minutes and he's carrying the only phone around on his belt. The tight security is part of Dr. Flagg's Sasquatch procedural manual."

"That's Flagg for you. He'll try to control it all." Buck ate a carrot. "Do you have a computer and modem?"

"Yeah."

"Is it still hooked up to a phone line?"

"I think so."

Buck went into the dining room and came back with a scrap of paper. "My E-mail address. Maybe we can communicate that way."

"Great idea!" All I had to do was sneak Dad into my room and show him how to send E-mail.

We sat for awhile in uncomfortable silence. The only sound was a clock ticking in the other room.

"Is there anything else, Dylan?"

This was my cue to leave, but I didn't get up. There were about a hundred things that I wanted to ask him. I picked up the photograph. "Is this your son?"

"Gary," Buck said quietly.

"Where does he live now?"

"He died right after that photo was taken."

"I'm sorry." I decided to skip the "how's your family?" chitchat.

Buck stood up. "Well, if that's everything . . ."

"Dad said you worked for the Fish and Wildlife Service."

"I was a field biologist, and when they thought I was too old for the field, they made me a desk biologist. I worked with endangered species, or as I liked to think of it, I worked *for* endangered species."

"What happened to your leg?"

"A fall," he said. "A long time ago, and it's not my leg. It's my hip. But I still manage to get around."

"Have you ever seen a Sasquatch, Buck? I mean aside from in your dreams."

He limped over to the front window, parted the blind, and peered outside.

"If you're thinking that your dad has lost his mind, you can relax—he hasn't."

"That's not what I asked."

He stepped away from the window. "There are a lot of things in the woods that we don't know about—things we don't want to know about. This is one of the reasons people live in towns and cities."

"You still haven't answered my question," I persisted.

"Would you believe me if I told you I had seen a Sasquatch? It's something you have to see for yourself. Even Dr. Flagg understands this. That's why he wants to kill one and bring it in."

"So, Dr. Flagg hasn't seen one either?"

Buck shook his head.

"Then why is he so sure that it exists?"

"Dr. Flagg is a man of great faith. That's about the only thing he has going for him. Now if you don't mind . . . I have a lot of things to do this afternoon. Tell your dad I'll need a map, and if he can swing it, one of their radios with the frequency they're going to use."

I got up and started toward the front door.

"Hold it," Buck said. "You better go out the same way you came in."

"I forgot." I wasn't looking forward to making my way back down the alley. He followed me into the kitchen. When I got to the backdoor I stopped. "So, why are you being watched, Buck?"

"That's still none of your business."

CHAPTER 7

WHEN I GOT HOME, Dad was in the kitchen making spaghetti. Joe West was sitting at the table reading the newspaper and eating a bowl of cereal as an appetizer before the main course. I could hear the television in the other room.

Joe looked up from the newspaper. "When does school get out?"

"Spring vacation's next week," I said.

"Nah, I mean what time of day does it get out."

"I don't know," I said. "A little after three. Why?" Dad stopped stirring the sauce.

Joe looked at his watch. "It's nearly five o'clock."

"So?"

"So, where have you been?"

"It's on!" someone shouted from the other room.

Joe ran into the living room.

"Saved by the news," Dad said quietly. "Are we set?"

"Buck said he would help."

"Good."

"These guys are really spooky, Dad."

"And getting spookier all the time, but there might be some good news on the television—at least for us and the Sasquatch."

The team was gathered around the television. A smoking Mount Saint Helens was on the screen, then they cut to the inside of a helicopter cockpit.

"It's too overcast to really see what's going on up here," the newscaster said from the chopper. *"But we understand from passing jets that they have seen smoke breaking through the clouds at 14,000 feet. There have been five minor quakes at roughly three hour intervals today. Volcanologists say it's only a matter of time before the mountain erupts."*

Back to the studio.

"To help us understand more about this impending volcanic eruption is our own volcanologist, Dr. Paul Smailes. Dr. Smailes, will this be similar to the 1980 eruption that killed fifty-seven people?"

"I don't think it is certain right now that the mountain is going to erupt."

The anchorman was obviously disappointed to hear this.

"Active volcanoes can spew steam and ash for fifty years without erupting," Dr. Smailes continued. *"This is how pressure is released. It doesn't necessarily mean impending disaster."*

I had the feeling that Dr. Smailes was not going to be asked to come back as their resident volcanologist. He was taking all the punch out of their lead story.

"*But the earthquakes, certainly they mean—*"

"*Seismic activity is perfectly normal in circumstances like these. There is always a tremendous amount of upheaval beneath the earth's crust. Earthquakes are simply a manifestation of this activity.*"

"*Thank you, Dr. Smailes . . .*"

In other words, you're fired, Dr. Smailes, I thought.

"*Authorities are in the process of establishing a red zone boundary to keep people away from the base of the mountain,*" the anchorman continued. "*Once the boundary has been set no one will be allowed in the area. Circling the red zone will be a blue zone. Only those with permits will be allowed in. Standing by with our mini-cam in the town of Toutle River is Melissa Otis. Melissa?*"

"*Hi Jeff, it's pretty peaceful along the Toutle river right now, but those of us who were here during the 1980 eruption know that this can change very quickly.*"

Melissa was about twenty-two years old, which meant she was five years old during the 1980 eruption. I doubted she remembered much about it.

"*What have you learned, Melissa?*"

"*The disaster committee is meeting right now in closed session to decide exactly where to establish both the red and*

87

blue zone boundaries. This will affect not only the area's full-time residents, but also the timber industry that this small rural community is so dependent upon. Officials are trying to avoid a repeat of the tragedy of the 1980 eruption where so many lives were lost. By the same token, they don't know if or when Mount Saint Helens will erupt and establishing these zones could have serious economic ramifications for Toutle and other small towns around the mountain.

"Another concern voiced earlier today by one official was the fact that spring vacation is starting next week for many schools. This could bring thousands of families to the mountain for a firsthand look. You might remember that during the 1980 eruption many sightseers had to flee for their lives—tragically some of them were killed."

The camera cut to 1980 footage of locals and tourists arguing with officials manning the roadblocks.

"If at all possible officials want to avoid a repeat of this kind of confrontation. The best thing to do is to stay away from the mountain for the time being."

"Looks like we'll be going up the mountain sooner than we thought," Dr. Flagg said. "We'll try to leave by tomorrow evening."

"We won't be ready," Clyde said.

"We have no choice. We must get up there before they establish the red and blue zones."

"What about the tracker?" Joe asked.

"He'll be here tomorrow morning."

What about me? I thought, but I didn't get a chance to ask because Dad and Dr. Flagg left in the red truck to pick up supplies in Eugene. Joe said they wouldn't be back until late.

About one o'clock in the morning I heard the truck pull into the driveway. Forty-five minutes later I heard Dad come up the stairs and go into his bedroom. I wanted to make certain that no one heard us, so I waited another fifteen minutes before sneaking across the hall and opening his door. The lights were off.

"Dad?" I whispered.

"What the . . . !" The light came on and Dr. Flagg came out of the bed like a jack-in-the-box. I was so startled I fell over backward. On my way down I grabbed the cord to the lamp and it crashed to the floor. Dr. Flagg yelled and feet pounded up the stairs. Joe West ran into the bedroom followed by Dad, Henry, Dean, and the Smithers. Someone flipped on the overhead light. Dr. Flagg was backed into the corner. He was pointing a pistol at me.

"What are you doing with that?" Dad shouted. He stepped in front of me.

"Sorry, Bill," Dr. Flagg said, lowering the pistol. "I didn't know it was your boy."

"Who did you think it was? You might have shot him!" I thought Dad was going to hit him. I had never seen him this mad.

"I apologized," Dr. Flagg said with an icy glare. They stared at each other. Flagg was the first to look away. He looked at me. "What are you doing in here?"

"I came in to talk to my dad."

"You should have knocked."

I stood up. "I didn't expect you to be in here."

Clyde explained what had happened in sign language to his brothers and the three of them went back downstairs along with Dean, Henry, and Joe West.

"Well," Dr. Flagg said, regaining his composure. "I suggest we all go back to bed. It was just a misunderstanding."

"It could have been a lot more than that," Dad said under his breath and followed me into my room, closing the door behind us. He sat down on the edge of the bed and covered his face with his hands for a few moments.

"Sorry, Dad, I didn't mean to cause a problem."

"It's not your fault. I had no idea Flagg slept with a gun. What's the matter with him?"

"I can think of about a thousand things."

Dad smiled and took a deep breath. He looked exhausted and I knew this was not the best time to bring it up, but I might not get another chance. "I want to go up to Mount Saint Helens with you."

"If it were just you and me that wouldn't be a problem, but I can't let you go up there with these maniacs. I don't know if you've noticed, but these guys are pretty intense. Flagg just pulled a gun on you!" He got up and started pacing.

"You have to understand that most of them have spent their whole adult lives searching for Sasquatch. They've been ridiculed and called insane. Bringing in a Sasquatch would change all that, to say nothing of the money they might make. Dylan, I don't know what's going to happen up there if they don't get their Sasquatch and I'm not going to put you in the middle of it."

"But you don't have any problem putting yourself in the middle of it," I said. He picked a great time to change from "mild" Bill Hickock to "wild" Bill Hickock. Why couldn't he have done this when Mom was here?

"Believe me," he said. "I'm having second thoughts, but it's too late to back out now. I'm not even sure if they would let me at this point."

"How could they stop you?"

He didn't say anything.

"What are you going to do if they find a Sasquatch?"

"I'm going to try to stop them from hurting it if I can. I'm hoping that Buck will be able to help me somehow."

"What am I supposed to do while you're on the mountain?"

"Stay at Doug's. I'm sure his parents will let you spend spring vacation over there. I'll call them tomorrow."

"I'll take care of it," I said quickly.

"Thanks." He ruffled my hair, which he hadn't done in a long time. "Don't worry about this, Dylan. We're going to go up there, see nothing, come back down, and it will be all over. The odds are in the Sasquatch's favor. No major expedition has ever seen a Sasquatch. All past sightings have been by pure chance."

"Why is Dr. Flagg sleeping in your room?"

"I told him he would be more comfortable in my bed and offered to use the couch. I wanted to try to get hold of that phone while Joe was asleep. I need to talk to Buck."

"Actually, he's waiting for you to E-mail him."

I turned my computer on and explained how to send and receive E-mail.

"That's all there is to it?" he asked after sending a message to Buck.

"That's it. Buck will probably respond by tomorrow morning."

He stood up. "When this is all over you'll have to show me more about this contraption."

"Sure."

After he left I stayed up for a long time thinking about what I was going to do. Staying at Doug's during spring vacation was not part of my plan.

I checked the E-mail before I left for school the next morning, but there was no word from Buck. When I got home Joe was at the table making a couple peanut-butter-and-pickle sandwiches. Dad and Dr. Flagg walked in.

"Did you talk to Doug's folks?" Dad asked.

"I'm all set."

"Good. Uncle John said he would come by this evening and take you over there."

What was he talking about? I didn't have an Uncle John.

"What time is he coming by?" Dr. Flagg asked.

"He said he thought he could make it by eight."

"Good," Dr. Flagg said. "We'll be gone by then." He walked out the back door with Joe close behind. The two peanut-butter-and-pickle sandwiches were gone. They would need a semi-truck to carry enough food for Joe to eat on the mountain.

"Who's Uncle John?"

"Mr. Johnson," Dad whispered. "Buck. He E-mailed me this morning. I put aside one of the radios. Dr. Flagg didn't realize that the triplets only need one radio between them. He won't miss it. It's in your top dresser drawer with a couple of extra batteries and a charger that can be plugged into a cigarette lighter. There's also a rough map of the area each team is responsible for."

"What about the tracker?"

"He's here. He flew in this morning and he hasn't said a word since he arrived—to anyone. He just sits in the living room chair and stares out the window. Scary."

"Who is he?"

"His name is Kurt Skipp."

"What about the red and blue zones? How are you going to get past the roadblocks?"

"They haven't established the zones yet, which is why Dr. Flagg wants to leave now. He wants to get in before they restrict access."

"What about the volcano?"

"I wish it would blow and shut this whole thing down, but it doesn't look like it's going to."

"What if it erupts when you're up there?"

"We'll be fine."

"Oh, yeah . . ."

Joe put his head through the back door. "Dr. Flagg needs you in the garage."

"I'll be right there," Dad said. Joe didn't budge. "Well, I'm sure you and Doug will have a good time."

"I'm sure we'll have a blast."

I swung through the living room to check out the new team member. He was sitting in a chair staring out the window just like Dad said. Next to him was a big green duffel bag and a long leather rifle-case. The Smithers had newspapers spread on the floor and were cleaning their rifles with solvent. If Mom saw this there would have been a *triplet homicide*.

I walked up to the man sitting in the chair and introduced myself. He swiveled his head toward me in slow motion. He was younger than I expected—mid-twenties or so. He wore a polo shirt, slacks, and brown loafers. His blond hair was short and carefully combed. He looked more like a video store clerk than a world-famous tracker. When his gray eyes finally reached mine they didn't blink. "Dylan Hickock," I repeated. He reached up and took my hand. His grip was gentle and his hand was surprisingly soft.

"Pleased to meet you, Dylan," he drawled. "My name is Kurt Skipp. Do you have an ironing board?"

At first I thought I hadn't heard him right.

"And spray starch?" he added.

"I think so. I'll have to look." I hadn't seen the ironing board since Mom started back at school.

"I need to press some things for the trip." He still had my hand.

"So, you're the tracker?" I asked, pulling my hand away.

"Yes."

"What do you do when you find what you're looking for?"

He glanced at the rifle-case. I guess the answer was inside of it.

"Where is the bathroom?"

He had sat in the chair all day without going to the bathroom? "It's right down the hall." I pointed.

"Thank you, Dylan."

"Are you hungry?" Maybe he had sat there all day waiting for someone to ask him if he needed anything.

"An apple would be nice, if you have one." He walked toward the bathroom—slowly. If he moved like this on Mount Saint Helens, the Sasquatch had nothing to fear.

I found the ironing gear in the back of a closet and set them up in the living room. Then I went to the kitchen to see if we had any apples. I kind of doubted it. Fruits and vegetables were things Mom bought, not Dad. But he surprised me—there was a bag of apples in the refrigerator along with some other vegetables. Mom would have been shocked.

Kurt had moved his duffel bag near the ironing board and was rummaging through it. He set out a pair of ankle-high hiking boots, thermal socks, gloves, and a jumpsuit made out of camouflage material. A real Rambo outfit.

"Here's your apple," I said. "Are you sure you don't want anything else? We have plenty of food."

"No, Dylan. This will be just fine." He held the apple in the palm of his left hand and looked at it like it was some kind of precious jewel. He reached into his pocket with his right hand and came out with a large folding knife made out of stainless steel. He flicked his wrist and the blade flipped open. There was a blur over the apple and the knife went back into his pocket in a single motion. "Would you like a slice?"

I didn't understand. The apple was still sitting on the palm of his hand—whole. He smiled, jiggled his hand, and the apple fell apart in four perfectly formed wedges. "Go ahead, Dylan, take one."

All I could do was stare. Kurt's legs might have been slow, but there was nothing slow about his hands. If he was as good with a rifle as he was with his little knife, Sasquatch was a dead cryptid. "I'm not hungry," I managed to say. "I've got to go up to my room and do some things."

"Well, it was nice to meet you, Dylan." Kurt put one

of the wedges into his mouth and crunched it.

When I got to my room I found the two-way radio and map in my drawer. With any luck these would be my ticket to Mount Saint Helens.

CHAPTER 8

I WATCHED THE EXPEDITION pull out of our driveway and head to the mountain. Their plan was to hide the vehicles, then hike to their designated starting points on foot. Dad and I didn't get another chance to talk before he left. As far as he knew, I was staying with Doug while he was gone.

After they pulled away, I went back inside and turned on the television. Mount Saint Helens was huffing and puffing, but no one seemed to know when or if it would blow. Officials were still arguing about where to put the red and blue zones, so access was still open.

I went out to the garage and started looking for my sleeping bag, which I had used exactly twice in my life during sleepovers with friends in our backyard. I didn't find it in the easy places and hoped Dad hadn't taken it with him. The only place left to look was the crawl space above the ceiling. I found a flashlight, lowered the ladder, and climbed up through the trap door. I was in luck:

the sleeping bag was in the corner, wrapped in plastic with about an inch of dust on it. I dropped it through the trapdoor and looked around for other stuff I might be able to use on the mountain. I found an old backpack that I didn't even know we owned. The only other things up there were boxes of notes from Dad's past tinkerings. I grabbed the pack and climbed down. I picked up the sleeping bag and started knocking the dust off.

"Going camping?"

The bag shot up into the air like a rocket and bounced off the ceiling, showering me with dust. Sitting in Dad's recliner was a man I had never seen before.

"What . . . Haaaa . . ." I started to sneeze.

The man waited for me to finish, then said, "Didn't mean to scare you, Dylan."

"Who are you?" I asked, wiping my nose. "What are you doing here? How do you know my name?"

"Actually I was looking for your father," he said calmly. "I rang your doorbell. No one answered so I came back here."

"And you thought it was okay to just walk in?"

"The door was unlocked."

The door to the garage had been broken for as long as I could remember. Dad was conscientious about fixing problems at his rental houses, but this did not carry over to our house. The man was the size of Joe West, but didn't have a beard and he was much older.

"Are you a friend of Dad's?"

"Never met him. Where is he?"

"He'll be here soon," I said.

"Good." He took off his rumpled hat and started to unbutton his heavy overcoat.

"What are you doing?"

"It's hot in here."

"Maybe you should come back later."

Hidden beneath the coat was a light blue shirt, a necktie, and a huge gut.

"I said you can't stay. You can give me your number and I'll give it to my dad."

"I'll wait."

I didn't have time for this. I had things to do. "If you don't leave I'm going to call the police."

He smiled, took out a black wallet from inside his coat, and flipped it open. Inside the wallet was a badge. Opposite the badge was an identification photo, which looked like him, but the picture was either twenty years old or else he had stolen his son's badge. But what really caught my attention was the name and the initials below the photo: Agent Steven Crow—Federal Bureau of Investigation. If he was actually an F.B.I. agent, he had been one for at least fifty years. "Go ahead," he said. "The number is 9-1-1."

"What do you want?"

He picked up one of Dad's books from the stand and leafed through it. "What's your father up to, Dylan?"

"He's a real estate agent." I said. And I thought back to how Dad had hidden his Sasquatch tinkering from Mom and me. Were there other things he was hiding? Things that the F.B.I. would be interested in?

"I'm not talking about his job," Agent Crow said. "There have been a lot of people over here the last few days. What were they doing?"

"Nothing," I said. Why was the F.B.I. watching our house?

"Do you know a man named Buckley Johnson?"

I looked at the gut sticking over his belt and I knew who he was. He was the man across the street who liked pizzas—a.k.a., Peter Nunn.

"He's one of my father's tenants," I said.

"What else do you know about him?"

"Not much."

He took a small spiral notebook out of his shirt pocket and flipped through the pages. "You and your dad had dinner with Buckley Johnson at Teter's restaurant last Friday. You ordered a hamburger, milk shake, large french fries, and pie with vanilla ice cream for dessert. What did you talk about at dinner?"

"He and my dad are both interested in cryptids."

"I beg your pardon?"

"Cryptids," I repeated. "Animals that are believed to exist but haven't been proven to exist."

"Oh yeah, like Bigfoot."

"Sasquatch."

"Whatever. So your old man is nuts like . . ."

"HE IS NOT!" I shouted. "There are a lot of undiscovered animals in the world. Last year they found seven previously unidentified primates in Brazil. Who are you to say . . . ?"

"Okay, okay." He held his hands up. "Simmer down. I didn't mean anything by that crack." He picked up one of Dad's cryptid journals and started leafing through it.

I took a deep breath, surprised at how mad I had gotten. A few days ago I probably would have agreed with Agent Crow about Bigfoot. "What's this have to do with the F.B.I.?"

He started to put the journal down and something slipped out from between the covers. It was one of Dad's maps. Agent Crow unfolded it. "What's this red X mean?"

Oh, that's the spot my dad saw Sasquatch a few months ago, I thought. I wasn't about to discuss that with an F.B.I. agent or anyone else. "Dad is always marking maps up."

"When did you say your dad would be back?"

"I'm not exactly sure."

"Right." He stood up and buttoned his coat.

"Has Mr. Johnson done something wrong?"

"We try not to waste our time watching innocent people. My advice is to stay away from him. Tell your dad that I was here and that I want to talk to him."

"How does he get in touch with you?"

He reached into his pocket. "I found these on your dad's workbench before you came down." He handed me the two Polaroid pictures Dad had taken the day we went to Buck's. "Tell him to drop by the house anytime. He has a key."

I stared at the Polaroids. I knew Dad should have skipped the photo session. When I looked up, Agent Crow was gone. I went over to the door and watched him back his green Ford Taurus out of the driveway. I had a feeling he wasn't going very far. The phone rang. I ran into the kitchen to get it.

"Are you alone?"

"Who is this?" I asked.

"Bigfoot! Who do you think it is?"

It was Buck. "I'm alone—now," I said.

"How long ago did he leave?"

"Agent Crow left about ten seconds ago. What's going on Buck?"

"Nothing's going on."

I waited. Buck sighed. "I don't know what he told you," he said impatiently. "But I don't have time to discuss it right now. I have to get up to that infernal mountain!"

"He's with the Federal Bureau of Investigation!"

"No he's not, but that doesn't matter right—"

"He had an F.B.I. badge!"

"He's not with the F.B.I., Dylan. Not anymore. He's a crackpot and I don't want him following me up to the mountain. Did your dad leave me the map and radio?"

"Yes."

"Crow is probably still watching your house. You'll need to sneak out and bring them to me."

"How did you know Agent Crow was here?"

"I drove by and saw his car in your driveway. I'll meet you downtown at Powell's City of Books. I'll be upstairs in the travel section, near the maps."

"I'm not coming until you tell me what's going on."

"Dylan, I need the map and radio. I can't help your father without them."

"And I need to know why Agent Crow is following you."

After a long pause Buck said, "Crow has been retired from the F.B.I. for as long as I've been retired from the Fish and Wildlife Service. He thinks I did something and he's been watching me on and off for years."

"What does he *think* you did?"

"He thinks I stole something."

"And did you?"

There was another long silence. "It was years ago," he said quietly. "I'm not going to tell you any more than that. If you don't want to give me the radio and map, I'll leave for the mountain right now without them. I have to get up there before they set up those restricted zones."

"I'll be there in an hour," I said.

I left several lights on in the house, hoping that Agent Crow would think I was still inside. I climbed the back fence and cut through our neighbor's yard. Powell's Books was downtown on west Burnside Street. I had been there hundreds of times with my parents. I hid in the bushes until the bus came, just in case Agent Crow happened to drive by.

Half an hour later I checked my backpack at the front counter. As usual Powell's was jammed with people. I went upstairs to the travel section. Buck wasn't there. I was about twenty minutes early, so I went to the cafe, got something to drink, and sat down at one of the tables.

By now, Dad was on Mount Saint Helens. I kept thinking about what he had said about this being the team's last chance. For most of them their whole lives would be defined by this trip to the mountain. If they succeeded in killing a Sasquatch, some people would hate them and some people would respect them, but regardless of how people felt they would go down in history as the guys who discovered the Sasquatch. If they failed, they would just be another group of crazies chasing a mythical beast. If Dad tried to stop them, what would they do?

I walked back up to the travel section. Buck was leaning on his staff near the maps with his hawk eyes darting all over the store.

"Were you followed?"

"I don't think so."

"Where's the map and radio?"

"I checked them at the counter with my pack."

"What do you mean your pack?"

"I'm going with you."

"Forget it."

"Then you can forget the map and radio."

"Your dad said that you were staying at a friend's house."

"I'm not going to sit in Portland while Dad is up on that mountain. If you don't take me, I'll go up there on my own."

Buck thought about this for a long time.

"How much time have you spent in the woods?"

"Basically none."

"So, if I let you go up there on your own and you get yourself killed it will be my fault." I didn't say anything. He looked at his watch. "I guess I'm too old to wrestle

107

the radio and map away from you. Let's get them and get out of here."

"Thanks, Buck."

"Believe me, you may not be thanking me when this is all over, and I'm certain your dad's not going to be happy about it."

I got my pack and followed him down the street to a battered Jeep Cherokee. He unlocked the driver's door, put his staff in the backseat, and got behind the wheel.

"There's no turning back now, Dylan."

I got in and we headed to the mountain.

CHAPTER 9

THEY WERE IN THE PROCESS of unloading the barricades to set up the restricted zone when we reached the mountain highway. No one stopped us.

"That was close," Buck said.

About a mile up the steep road we started to see fir trees dusted with gray ash from the volcano.

"Why don't you make yourself useful and see if we can pick our friends up on that radio."

I dialed in the frequency they were using and listened. Nothing.

"They're probably bedded down for the night," Buck said.

"Where are we going to stay?"

"I have a spot all picked out. At least for tonight."

Soon, the entire road was covered with a thick layer of ash. Buck pulled the Jeep over and shut off the engine.

"Is there a problem?"

"There should be a roll of toilet paper in the glove box," Buck said. "And a flashlight."

"Oh." I found them in the cluttered compartment.

Buck got out, but instead of heading into the bushes, he popped the Jeep's hood. I got out to see if I could help.

"Hold this." He handed me the flashlight. "If I don't wrap this air filter with toilet paper the ash will clog it up and we won't be going anywhere." When he finished he put the filter back into the slot and slammed the hood closed.

"I might as well pee," I said.

"While you're doing that, I'll take a look at the team locations. Where's that map?"

I wasn't sure if I should give him the map or not. The only thing I really knew about Buck was that he was being watched by an ex–F.B.I. agent.

"What's the matter? Are you afraid I'll drive off and leave you here?"

"I don't know."

"Well, I won't. I didn't want you along, but you're here now and that's the way it is. You're not going to be much help to your father or the Sasquatch unless you stop this nonsense and start trusting me."

I gave him the map, but I took the radio with me.

When I finished I stood there for a few moments and looked around. We were parked near the edge of a sharp drop-off. The only things I could see clearly were the silhouettes of tall fir trees swaying in the brisk wind and a few small patches of snow that weren't covered in ash. The sound of frogs and crickets filled the cool night. Suddenly, the crickets and frogs stopped singing. There was a low rumbling noise. The sound got louder and the ground began to roll as if I were standing on the deck of a boat. I lost my balance and fell to my hands and knees.

"Dylan!" Buck shouted.

"I'm here!"

He found me with the flashlight beam. "Get away from the edge!"

The ground was rolling too much for me to stand, so I crawled on my hands and knees toward the Jeep. About halfway there the tremor stopped as suddenly as it had started. I got to my feet. Buck came over. "You all right?"

"I guess so," I said, although my legs were still shaking.

"You'll get used to the quakes. There were something like 10,000 of them in the months leading up to the 1980 eruption. What you just felt was nothing more than the mountain belching. A little indigestion is all."

Somehow I didn't find this very comforting.

"Let's get the radio out and see if it woke up your dad and the others."

I turned the radio on. There was static, then Flagg's voice came over the radio. . . .

"This is Unit One, radio check."

"Unit Two here. That sure woke us up!"

"Unit Three. We read you loud and clear."

"Can you see any volcanic activity from your locations? Over."

"Negative, One. It's too dark to see anything."

"Same here, One. Too dark."

"I copy that. I'll check back in at O-six-hundred. Over and out."

I wondered what Dad thought of the mountain belching, and whether he was having second thoughts about this whole thing. I know I was. My legs were still quivering.

"Sounds like the gang's all here," Buck said and climbed back into the Jeep.

An hour later he slowed the Jeep down and turned onto an overgrown dirt road that didn't look like it had been used in years.

"Up ahead is a chain." He flipped the visor down and handed me a key. "You'll have to unlock it. Don't bother putting it back up. If we need to get out of here in a hurry I don't want anything to slow us down."

When we got to the chain I unlocked it and we started up a steep incline. The road was so narrow the brush scraped both sides of the Jeep. After two jarring miles we leveled off and came to a stop in front of an ancient log cabin.

"Home sweet home," Buck said.

"The cabin's yours?"

"Yep."

"I thought everything up here was destroyed by the 1980 eruption. This cabin has been here a lot longer than that."

"About a hundred years longer," Buck said. "Aside from dumping a ton of ash on it, the mountain left it alone. I thought I was going to be toast."

"You were here during the eruption?" Buck got out of the Jeep and walked around to the back without answering. I jumped out and followed him. "You were here?"

"No reason to shout, Dylan. Yes, I was here."

"Why?"

"I had my reasons. Give me a hand with this stuff."

I grabbed an armload of gear and followed him, intending to ask what it was like during the eruption, but the stench inside the cabin obliterated that notion. It almost knocked me over. It smelled like a bunch of skunks had thrown a party inside. "What is that?"

"Stale air. It will air out in awhile."

It was more than stale air. If it didn't go away I was sleeping outside. Buck lit a couple of kerosene lanterns.

"No electricity?"

Buck shook his head. "And we have to haul water up from the stream. This is how people used to live, Dylan. Let's get these windows open."

"Won't the ash blow in?" My eyes were still itching from our first stop on the mountain.

"It's either ash or stink. You choose."

I chose ash.

The inside of the one-room cabin wasn't much to look at. There were small windows along three walls. Running the length of the remaining wall was a fireplace made out of round river stones. Across from the fireplace was a counter and sink and a rusty woodstove. In the center of the room were two army cots without mattresses, a rickety table, and three mismatched chairs. Along the remaining wall was a wooden storage locker. It was at least twelve feet long and four feet wide. I walked over to it. The hinged top was two inches thick and had big padlocks on the front and on both sides. "What's this?"

"Pandora's box," Buck said.

"Seriously, what's in it?"

"Supplies. I keep it locked in case a bear gets in here. Why don't you go out and get the rest of the gear while I start a fire."

It took me three trips to get everything inside. On the last trip I brought Buck's walking staff with me. He had a fire going in the fireplace and was loading the wood stove with paper and kindling. I took a close look at the walking staff in the lantern light. Besides the Sasquatch face there were also human faces carved on the stick. I thought I recognized his wife and son. The top of the stick was a mountain. "Is this Mount Saint Helens?"

"Yes." He closed the door to the woodstove without lighting it.

"How long have you been carving?"

"Since I was a boy."

"You're good. Is this your wife and son?"

"Yeah." He took the stick and put it over in the corner.

"Did you injure your hip when Mount Saint Helens erupted?"

"No, that happened a long time before that. But let's stop the interview, Dylan."

"I was just curious."

"I know," he said. "But we have more important things to discuss than my life story."

Buck was a bigger mystery than the Sasquatch. I had a feeling he knew a lot more about them than he was saying. "So, what's our plan?"

"Now, that's a legitimate question." He sat down on one of the cots. "Years ago when I was still in the field we had this technique for dealing with problems we weren't exactly sure how to solve. We called it S-W-A-G."

"What's that stand for?"

"Scientific-Wild-Ass-Guess—meaning we're just going to have to take care of problems as they come up. If we're lucky they won't find any sign of the Sasquatch and go home. Let's get some sleep. I have a feeling we're going to need it."

The scream woke me. My eyes snapped open and I sat up. "What was that?"

"Mountain lion," Buck said calmly.

The sound came again. It was loud and guttural—more like an angry roar than a scream. I had a feeling that it was coming from some distance off, which meant that it was very loud.

"There's no way that's a mountain lion."

"Oh really? How many mountain lions have you heard?"

"None," I admitted.

Buck snorted. "Didn't think so. Don't worry about

it. The cat can't get inside. Go back to sleep."

I lay there half the night with my eyes wide-open. Whatever made the sound didn't do it again. But I was convinced that it wasn't a mountain lion.

CHAPTER 10

BUCK WAS BANGING AROUND in the kitchen as the first rays of morning light came through the windows. I wanted to sleep for a week, but I swung my legs out of the cot and put my feet on the cold wooden floor.

"You like pancakes?" Buck asked.

"Sure."

"Good. Go down to the stream and get some water and I'll make you as many as you can shovel into your mouth."

I got dressed and went outside. Everything was gray— the ground, the trees, even the sky. The ash had turned the normally green landscape into a black and white photo. I found a stack of five-gallon buckets, poured the ash from one of them, and started off, then realized that I had no idea where the stream was. I was going to shout at Buck and ask him, but decided not to. If I couldn't find a stream on my own, I shouldn't be on the mountain trying to help my crazy father. I found a narrow trail and followed it downhill through the thick Douglas firs.

About two hundred yards from the cabin I began to have doubts about my choice. With his bad hip, it wouldn't be easy for Buck to haul water this far.

I was about ready to turn back when I remembered the terrible roaring scream from the night before. My heart started pounding in my chest like a jackhammer. I don't know how, but I knew this is where the sound had come from. Mountain lion. That's what Buck said it was, but I still had my doubts.

I started back up the trail a lot faster than I had come down. I looked at the ground, telling myself that I was checking for cat tracks, but what I was really doing was trying not to look off into the dark trees because of what I might see there. I was about halfway back to the cabin when I saw the first track. It didn't belong to a cat.

I stared down at the deep impression in the gray ash in shock. It had to be over twenty inches long and at least eight inches wide. The toes were the size of golf balls. About four feet away was another track with my boot print right in the middle of it. The footprints were heading down the trail where I had just been.

The bucket dropped from my hand. I didn't see any other footprints on my way back to the cabin because I was running too fast. I burst through the cabin door.

"Sa . . . Sa . . . as . . ." I put my hands on my knees and tried to catch my breath. A few moments later I managed to complete the word, "Sasquatch!"

Buck calmly put another log in the woodstove as if I had just reported seeing a squirrel. "Did you get the water?"

"Did you hear what I said?" I shouted. "I just saw this huge footprint on the trail. It was just like the photographs in Dad's books. And it wasn't more than a football field away from here. I'm talking huge!"

"And I'm talking water," Buck said. "I can't make pancake batter without it. I don't know about you, but I'm hungry."

I stared at him. This was not the reaction I expected. "It wasn't a mountain lion last night."

"No."

"Why did you lie to me?"

"Because if I told you it was a Sasquatch you would have been up all night irritating me with questions."

"I notice you didn't have any trouble sleeping after you heard the sound."

"That's not the first time I've heard it."

"What's happening here, Buck? We're not going to be much help to my dad or the Sasquatch unless you stop this nonsense and start trusting me."

Buck laughed. "Seems like I've heard that somewhere before." He looked out the window. "Okay, Dylan. The Sasquatch are real. You just saw a footprint and look how upset you are. Imagine your dad's shock when he actually saw the beast."

"So, you've seen the Sasquatch."

"Many, many times."

"What was that sound last night? It sounded like it was angry to me."

"Frustrated, is more like it. The Sasquatch get upset when there are strangers in the woods, especially if there's a stranger with me."

"Are you saying that it knows I'm here?"

"Of course it knows you're here. Last night it was probably standing in the trees watching you unload the Jeep."

I sat down on my cot. This was way too weird for me. Buck was too calm about all this. He was acting like he was a close personal friend of the Sasquatch. "So, how many Sasquatch are out here?"

"I don't know," Buck said quietly. "Three is the most I've ever seen together. But that was years ago and one of them was a youngster."

"A baby Sasquatch?"

"Four or five years old. I don't know how many are out here. A dozen, maybe more."

"So, what are they?"

"More human than ape. Beyond that I don't know. I do know that they are harmless. I'm not . . ."

The cabin began to shake. Buck fell down. The cot I was sitting on slid across the floor and banged into the woodstove. The pipe came loose and smoke started pouring into the cabin. I jumped off the cot and was about to grab the pipe and try to put it in the hole in the ceiling when Buck yelled, "No, Dylan! It's too hot!" I snatched my sleeping bag off the dancing cot. The tremor stopped just as I wrapped the sleeping bag around the stove pipe. I got the pipe back in the ceiling without any problem, but the cabin was already filled with smoke.

"Let's get out of here," Buck said between coughs.

I helped him through the door. When we got outside we both fell to our knees and gulped in fresh air.

"Now that was a shaker!" Buck said.

"Maybe it was the eruption."

"I don't think so. When the smoke clears, go into the cabin and get the two-way radio. And while you're at it grab my staff."

I waited a few minutes, then went back inside and found the staff and the radio.

Flagg's voice came over the radio as soon as Buck turned it on.

"*Repeat that, Unit Two.*"

"*We can see some smoke or ash from here, but other than that it seems okay.*"

"Roger, Two. Unit Three? . . .Unit Three, do you read me?"

"Who's in Unit Three?" Buck asked.

"The triplets."

"Get the map. I want to see where they're supposed to be."

One good thing about the woodstove accident was that it seemed to dilute the bad smell inside the cabin. When I came back with the map, Clyde was on the radio.

". . . Everything is fine here, Unit One. Unit Three out."

Buck switched the radio off. "If that quake didn't scare the fools off the mountain, nothing will." He spread the map on the ground.

"Where are we?" I asked.

"Here." Buck pointed. It looked like Clyde's area was about ten miles away from us. The other teams were within two or three miles of him.

"You were telling me about the Sasquatch when the quake hit."

"I was about to say that I wasn't going to tell you anything more about the Sasquatch when the quake hit." He folded up the map and used his staff to get to his feet. "But I'll make a deal with you if you promise not to pester me anymore about it."

"I can't promise until I know what the deal is."

"Then forget it." He started toward the cabin.

"Okay," I said. "I promise."

"Good." He stopped and turned around. "You go get that water and I'll tell you about the Sasquatch over breakfast. That's about how long it will take for me to tell you everything I know. After that, not another question about them. Deal?"

"I'll try."

He grinned. "Well, at least you're honest."

"Where's the stream?"

"That way." He pointed in the opposite direction from which I had gone earlier. "About fifty yards. You can't miss it. There's water in it."

He handed me another bucket.

Buck was right, it didn't take him long to tell me about his experiences with the Sasquatch. Although, I suspected he wasn't telling me everything.

When Buck was a field biologist he was assigned to Mount Saint Helens. In all his years exploring the mountain he had never even seen a Sasquatch footprint until he met Billy Taylor, the previous owner of the cabin.

"When I had my fall, it was Billy Taylor who got me back on my feet. At the time, he had been living like a hermit up here for nearly fifty years. He didn't have a car, and as far as I know he rarely left the woods. I think he had gotten into some kind of trouble with the law and he just faded into the wilderness. He hunted and fished to keep himself alive. I couldn't walk, so without transportation I was stranded up here with him.

"One night I was looking out the window and saw my first Sasquatch standing about where we are right now. The moon was full and I could see the animal clear as daylight, but I still thought I was having some kind of hallucination.

"I told Billy there was some kind of giant standing in front of his cabin. He nodded, got up from the table, and walked outside. I would have tried to stop him, but I couldn't even get out of bed because of my hip. I watched through the window as he stood not three feet away from the Sasquatch. It towered over him and it looked like Billy was using some kind of sign language to communicate with it. After about ten minutes the Sasquatch turned and walked away. Billy came back inside and sat down at the table as if nothing had happened.

"'What was that?' I asked him.

"'A neighbor,' he said.

"Billy refused to talk about the incident. Over the next few weeks I was glued to that window, hoping for another glimpse of the beast. It didn't come back though. My hip finally healed up and I was able to hobble down the hill and get help.

"I didn't tell anybody about what I had seen. My colleagues in the Fish and Wildlife Service would have thought I broke my head, not my hip. Six months after I got back, an attorney contacted me. Billy Taylor had died and left me this cabin. I used to come here a lot. It took awhile for the Sasquatch to get used to me, but eventually they started coming around. I don't encourage them and I don't discourage them. I've been up here for a month and not seen a single sign. Other times they come around every night.

"I haven't been able to get up here much in the last few years. This hip is hurting me a lot more these days. Old age is a terrible thing."

"You seem to get around pretty well."

"It's just an act," he said.

His story left me with more questions than I had had before he started. Weren't there people out looking for him when he disappeared? His wife, Betty, must have gone out of her mind with worry. How did Billy learn to communicate with the Sasquatch? But I didn't ask because I promised I wouldn't.

Buck limped into the trees and came back a few minutes later with a stout branch. He set it on the porch, went inside for a minute, came back out with a chair, and sat down. I thought he was going to carve another walking staff, but instead he spent the afternoon whittling the branch down to nothing.

PART THREE

THE MYTH

And he opened the bottomless pit, and there arose a smoke out of the pit, like the smoke of a great furnace; and the sun and the air were darkened by reason of the smoke of the pit.

—Revelation 9:2

CHAPTER 11

A COLD, STEADY RAIN kept us inside the cabin for the next few days.

Buck and I fell into a set routine. We woke at dawn. I went down to the stream and got water. Buck made pancakes. I washed the dishes. Buck went out and found a fir branch and brought it inside. While we monitored the team's conversations on the two-way, Buck turned the branch into a toothpick and I played solitaire with the filthiest deck of cards I had ever seen. There were two cards missing, which made it impossible to win. For added entertainment, we listened to Buck's portable radio to find out when and if the mountain would explode. For dinner Buck heated up canned stew or chili. For dessert we ate raw carrots. A couple of real mountain men.

I wasn't sleeping well because of the nightmare. I dreamed I was running up a wooden stairway trying to get away from a monster. As I ran up the stairs the monster grabbed my ankles and dragged me away. This was not the first time I'd had this nightmare. It was a rerun from when I was a kid that started after an evening of werewolf videos at Doug's house. I hadn't had the dream in several years and there was a new twist this time around. Just before I started running up the stairs, the monster screamed. The sound was a lot like the roar we heard on the first night, but muffled somehow, as if it were coming through my pillow. I knew I was having a nightmare, but the scream sounded real. When I awoke I expected the scream to continue, but all I heard were the frogs croaking, Buck's breathing, and the wind blowing through the trees.

The newscasters were still saying the big eruption was imminent. They assured us that the entire mountain had been evacuated and everything was secure. Boy, did I have a news scoop for them!

I lost track of how many times the ground shook. None of the tremors were as bad as the one that moved my cot across the floor, but all of them scared me. I thought that each rumble was the final belch before the mountain blew.

The teams had not found a single track and we could tell by their voices that they were getting discouraged, which was exactly the way we wanted it.

"Couple more days of this and they'll give it up," Buck predicted.

The morning of the third day started out with a huge quake. I was down at the stream getting water when it hit. I fell to the ground and held on like I was going to fall off the planet. When it stopped I ran back to the cabin to see if Buck was okay. He was sitting at the kitchen table with the map spread out, listening to the radio.

"Are you all right?"

"Fine." Buck pointed to the radio.

"Unit Two, have you heard from Unit Three this morning?"

"Flagg has been trying to get ahold of Clyde's team since you left for the stream," Buck said.

"Negative," Joe said.

"Maybe the spaceship picked them up," Henry commented.

"This is no joke!" Flagg snapped. *"Losing contact is serious."*

"I heard that, Henry!" It was Clyde. He sounded out of breath. *"We thought we saw something in a ravine and we were on our way down to investigate when that quake hit. We nearly killed ourselves getting to the bottom. I lost the radio signal down there and I scrambled back up here to tell you what we were doing. My brothers are still in the ravine looking around."*

"What did you see?" asked Flagg.

"Something moving along the bottom. I don't know what it was. It was too brushy and too far away to see clearly, but we could hear branches breaking down there. Big branches. It sounded like firecrackers going off."

"Maybe it was a tree falling," Flagg suggested. "Or a grizzly bear crashing around."

"It doesn't take five minutes for a tree to fall, Dr. Flagg. And we have black bears in this neck of the woods, not grizzly bears. A black bear is too small to crack branches as big as we heard. No, it was something else."

"Where is this ravine?"

Clyde mentioned a few landmarks and Buck pointed to the spot on the map.

"I'm going to go back down and see what I can find," Clyde said.

"Stay in radio contact. If you see anything, notify us immediately."

"Like I told you, Dr. Flagg, the radio doesn't work down in the ravine. The best I can do is check in when I get back up. Out."

"Clyde? Are you still out there? Clyde?"

Clyde didn't answer. I could almost see Flagg's fury. They had only been searching for a few days and already he was starting to lose control of his teams. I had an urge to grab the radio and ask how Dad was doing. I was sure he was fine, but I hadn't heard his voice since he backed the red tank out of the driveway three days earlier. It was strange knowing he was less than ten miles away from us and I couldn't talk to him.

"What do you think Clyde heard in that ravine?" I asked.

Buck looked worried. "I don't know."

"Have you been down in that ravine?"

"A couple of times."

"So, is he on to something? Do the Sasquatch hang out down there?"

"The Sasquatch hang out wherever they want to."

That evening when Clyde checked in, Flagg told him he wanted him to move out of the ravine the following morning and continue searching his assigned area.

"*Negative on that!*" Clyde said. "*We're not done with the ravine. Not by a long shot.*"

"*We have a lot of ground to cover, Clyde. I don't know how much time we have. If you haven't found anything down there by now, you're not going to find anything.*"

"*I know something's here! I feel it in my gut.*"

"*Give it up and move on,*" Flagg said. "*After you finish searching your area you can go back to the ravine if there's time.*"

"*No way, Flagg! If you heard what we heard you'd have everyone down there looking around. I think it's laying low*" *waiting for us to leave. I'm going back down. I'll check in with you tomorrow evening. Out . . ."*

Things got worse for Flagg on the fourth morning. Joe's team was listening to the new reports as they searched for a sign of the Sasquatch. Every time they heard something about the impending eruption their radios started crackling with conversation. Flagg told them to stop listening to the news reports.

"If you're listening to the news you're not paying attention," he said. *"And the sound of the radio might scare Sasquatch off."*

"We listen through earphones," Joe said.

"If the Sasquatch's hearing is that good, it can hear us stomping through the woods from miles away," Dean added.

"Especially Joe," Henry said.

"Actually, a female Sasquatch might think he's cute and come running," Dean said with a laugh.

"Enough of that!" Flagg snapped. *"We don't have time for jokes. There's too much at stake. I shouldn't have to tell you how important this is. I know the weather's bad and we haven't seen anything, but we still have to approach this search like professionals."*

"You forgot to mention the volcano, Dr. Flagg," Henry pointed out. *"We could be buried anytime. We're just*

blowing off steam—there's nothing wrong with that. It's just our way of easing tension."

"Well," Flagg said. *"I would prefer you ease your tension off radio and leave the channel open for more important communications."*

This stopped the idle chatter for an hour, then Joe came on the radio . . . *"This whole thing is ridiculous! No intelligent animal in its right mind is going to be wandering around an active volcano. We would be better off coming back after the mountain settles down."*

"Which means that Joe's running out of food," Buck said with a laugh.

Flagg didn't answer Joe right away. I'm sure he was a little shocked that his most faithful follower was starting to waver. *"I hear you, Joe. I guess we should get together and talk face-to-face. We'll finish our sweeps today and meet above the ravine. Five o'clock sound good to everyone?"*

"Why the ravine?" Dean asked.

"Because we're all about an equal distance away from it. Except for Clyde and his brothers, of course."

When Buck heard this he cursed and buried the blade of his knife into the table.

"What's the matter?" I asked. It seemed to me this was good news. They might just call off the expedition and we could all go home.

"If they're together they won't be using their radios

and we'll have no idea what they're up to! Why did they have to pick the ravine to meet at?"

"What difference does it make?"

Buck didn't answer me. He limped outside and slammed the door behind him.

There was something about this ravine Buck wasn't telling me. He had been very tense ever since Clyde and his brothers had gone down there. About ten minutes later Buck came back in dragging another fir branch.

"Any more chatter?" he asked.

"No," I said. "But I was thinking. Maybe we should go down to the ravine—get close enough to their camp to hear what they're saying."

"Hah! I wouldn't get within a mile of those gun-toting maniacs. Have you forgotten why they're up here? If they see a movement they can't explain—*BLAM!*" He started in on the branch.

I finished the dishes and was about to pick up the deck of cards when I saw a bright shaft of sunlight come through the window. It had stopped raining.

"I'm going for a walk," I announced.

Buck didn't look up from the branch.

CHAPTER 12

AFTER THE RAIN, the Douglas firs were bright green against the blue sky and the air was crisp and clear. If it weren't for the sticky gray ash on the ground I wouldn't have known that I was on the slope of an active volcano.

I knew where I wanted to go, but I wasn't sure if I could make myself go there. I couldn't get those huge footprints in the ash out of my mind, and yet I never wanted to see them again. I knew why Dad had not gone back to where he had seen the Sasquatch. And I knew why Flagg and the others were so obsessed with finding the beast. I walked over to the trail and stopped.

"Don't be a coward, Dylan!" I told myself.

If I wanted to learn more about the Sasquatch I was going to have to do it on my own. Buck certainly wasn't going to help me. I started down the trail. The ground was slippery and I had to hold onto branches on the steeper spots to keep from falling. When I got to the place where I had left the bucket I stopped and looked for tracks, but the rain had washed them all away.

I sat down on the bucket and tried to recall the terror I felt when I saw those footprints, but I couldn't bring it back. Birds were chirping and flitting from tree to tree, a squirrel dug into the carpet of pine needles looking for seeds—just another peaceful day in the woods. Nothing to be afraid of . . .

SNAP!

I nearly fell off the bucket. Just a limb breaking off a tree, I told myself, but somehow I knew it wasn't.

SNAP!

I stood up. Whatever was snapping those branches was big. And it was coming my way. Clyde had described a similar snapping sound down in the ravine. I thought about running back to the cabin. *SNAP!* But what would I do when I got to the steep part of the trail? It would be like trying to scramble up a greased slide. *SNAP!* I looked for a place to hide. About twenty feet off the trail was a big moss-covered log. I clambered over the top of it and crouched down on the other side. An eerie quiet settled over the woods. I heard the crunch of footsteps coming up the trail. The steps stopped directly across from where I was hiding. I heard the bucket being moved and I imagined the Sasquatch looking down at my footprints in the wet ash just as I had looked down at its footprints a few days earlier. The only difference was that it didn't run off like I had. It

138

just stood there. I heard it breathing. There was a slight wheezing sound with each intake of air. As the seconds went by, the wheezing seemed to lessen. Finally the footsteps continued up the trail toward the cabin. I waited, then very, very slowly raised my head above the log. I wasn't about to let my chance to see a Sasquatch slip by, even if it meant I would only see its backside. At least I hoped I only saw it from behind.

The creature I saw walking up the trail was big, but it wasn't a Sasquatch. I stood up. "What are you doing up here?" I shouted.

Agent Crow whipped around with surprising speed. He had a pistol in his hand. I dove behind the log. It seemed like everybody was pointing a pistol at me these days.

"It's me, Dylan Hickock!" I peeked over the top of the log.

"Are you crazy?" Crow yelled. "I might have blown your head off!"

"I noticed." I climbed back over the log.

He put the pistol under his coat, sat down on the bucket, and began wheezing again. "You scared the . . ." He took a deep breath. "Man, you shouldn't be sneaking up on people like that."

"I didn't expect to see an F.B.I. agent out here."

"Why were you hiding?"

I was too embarrassed to tell him, so I changed the

139

subject. "How did you know Buck was up here?"

"A hunch. I've known about his cabin for years. When he didn't come home I figured he must be on the mountain."

"So, you've been here before?"

"A few times."

Agent Crow looked pretty bad. His fleshy face was pale and shiny with sweat, despite the cool temperature. His clothes were wrinkled and streaked with ash. He was wearing an overcoat, slacks, dress shirt, and wing-tip shoes. No tie. Not exactly the best attire for tromping around the woods. "How long have you been up here?" I asked.

"Couple of days."

"Where have you been sleeping?"

"In my car."

"How did you get past the barricades?"

"My badge." He reached into his coat pocket and came out with a two-way radio. "Is your dad with them?"

I didn't see any point in denying it. I nodded.

"So, what are they doing?"

"If you've been listening, then you know exactly what they're doing."

"They're looking for Bigfoot."

"Sasquatch," I said.

"Whatever. And Johnson's helping them?"

"He's trying to stop them. So is my dad."

"Stop them from what?"

"From hurting an animal that just wants to be left alone. Why are you following Buck?"

"I guess we all have to follow something." He stared off into the woods for a few moments, then looked at me. "You don't know Buckley Johnson very well, do you?"

"No," I said. "But I trust him."

"Well, let me fill you in on a few details. For instance, did you know that your trusted friend hijacked an airplane on November 24, 1971?"

"No way!"

"At the Portland Airport he boarded Northwest Airlines flight 305 bound for Seattle and told the ticket agent his name was Dan Cooper.

"The Boeing 727 took off at 4:45 P.M. with twenty-four passengers. A few minutes after takeoff, he gave the flight attendant a note that said he had a bomb in his briefcase. He wanted $200,000 in twenty-dollar bills and four parachutes to be delivered to him when the airplane landed in Seattle."

"I don't believe you," I said.

"Let me get this straight. You believe in Bigfoot, but you don't believe this? Amazing. Want me to continue?"

I nodded.

"The captain went back to talk to him about the alleged bomb. Johnson opened the briefcase long enough for the captain to glimpse two large red cylinders and a jumble of wires. It probably wasn't a bomb, but we didn't want to take any chances. We decided to meet Johnson's demands—there wasn't time to do anything else. Ten thousand twenty-dollar bills were bundled into hundred-bill stacks and put into a canvas bank bag.

"Flight 305 landed in Seattle at 5:40 P.M. The captain asked if the passengers could be let go. Johnson said yes, but the cockpit crew and one flight attendant were to remain on the airplane.

"When the passengers were safely off, the money and four parachutes were given to the flight attendant. She asked Johnson if he was going to make somebody jump with him. He said he might.

"Johnson told the captain to fill the airplane with fuel and take off for Mexico City. The captain said they would have to stop on the way to refuel. They settled on stopping in Reno, Nevada. He told the captain not to exceed a speed of 150 knots. The cabin was to remain unpressurized. They were to fly at or below an altitude of 10,000 feet. Johnson said he had an altimeter to keep track of their altitude.

"At 7:46 P.M. the 727 took off again and headed for

Reno. We sent up two F-106 fighter jets to follow the airplane and report what they saw.

"Johnson ordered the flight attendant to go to the cockpit and shut herself in with the crew. At about 8 P.M. a red light appeared on the engineer's panel in the cockpit. It was the 'open door' warning. At 8:10 the airplane passed over the Lewis River on the south side of Mount Saint Helens. The two jets lost visual contact with the airplane because they couldn't fly slowly enough.

"When the airplane landed in Reno at 10:15 P.M. we were there to meet it, but Johnson wasn't on the airplane.

"The news media erroneously reported the hijacker's name as D. B. Cooper. It didn't matter though, because his name wasn't D. B. Cooper, or Dan Cooper. His name was Buckley Johnson."

I stared at Agent Crow. "Buck couldn't have jumped from a jet. He has a bad hip."

"How do you think he hurt his hip?"

Buck told me he had injured it in a fall. But he didn't say he fell 10,000 feet! I still couldn't believe that the old man up in the cabin was capable of hijacking an airplane.

"What did he do with the money?"

"I have no idea. We recovered about $6,000 in 1980. A kid found three bundles of twenties in the sand along the Columbia River near Vancouver. I don't know how it got there, but it had been there for a long time."

"If you were so sure he did it, why didn't you arrest him?"

"Johnson was one of our primary suspects, but we didn't have enough hard evidence for a conviction."

"Why was he a suspect?"

"We checked out everyone in Portland with skydiving or military jump training. Johnson fit the bill—he was a paratrooper during the Korean War. When we went to Johnson's house to interview him, his wife said that he had left her and she didn't know if he would ever be back. We checked into it and found out that his son, Gary, was in the hospital dying from bone marrow cancer. It didn't add up. Johnson didn't seem the type to abandon his wife and son. We asked his wife for a recent photograph of him—she said there weren't any, that Johnson was camera shy. We got a search warrant and we couldn't even find a baby picture. I think she ditched them."

I hadn't seen any photos of him at the house either, which seemed a little odd now that I thought about it.

"Johnson came back home a couple months after the boy died. He told us he had been down in Mexico looking for some kind of cure for his son. He claimed that he got hit by a car down there and broke his hip. He said an old man picked him up off the road and took him to his house. He stayed there several months while his hip healed."

"Did you check his story with the man that took him in?" I asked.

Agent Crow shook his head. "Johnson said he had no idea who the man was, or even where he lived. He was hit at night in a rural area. The man took him to his house up in the hills. He didn't speak English and Johnson didn't speak Spanish. When Johnson's hip got better the mystery man drove him to San Diego and dropped him off without a word.

"We put Johnson in a lineup and had the passengers and crew come in for a look at him, but they couldn't pick him out. Dan Cooper had dark brown hair, Johnson had blond hair. He probably dyed it when he hijacked the airplane, but it grew out by the time we got him in the lineup. Also, Johnson had lost a lot of weight during the months he was gone. Anyway, we couldn't prove he was Dan Cooper, so we had to let him go. End of story."

"Except you didn't believe him."

"Not for a second. Johnson was taken off the suspect list and I was transferred to the East Coast. When I retired a few years ago I moved back out here and picked up where we left off."

"If nobody was hurt and he didn't spend the money,

what's the point after all these years? He's just an old man now."

"Buckley Johnson hijacked that airplane," Agent Crow said. "And the last time I checked, that was still against the law."

"So, why are you up here? Do you think he has the money stashed in the cabin or something?"

"I've searched the cabin a dozen times. It's not there. Johnson either spent the money or dumped it. I came up here to see what he was doing. Now, I'm going to leave before the mountain erupts and I suggest you do the same thing. I was just coming up the trail for one last look."

I didn't like the way that sounded.

"You've got yourself hooked up with a bunch of real kooks, son. I'll give you a ride out of here if you want. We can stop and pick up your dad on the way."

I was tempted, but I knew Dad wouldn't come with us. "I think they might call the expedition off tonight," I said.

"I think you're making a mistake." Agent Crow said. "I just hope the volcano holds out long enough for you to get out of here."

"I'll be okay."

"Well, when you see Johnson give him my regards and watch out for that Bigfoot." Agent Crow laughed and started back down the trail.

I stayed there for a while thinking about the hijacking. Maybe Buck had lied to Agent Crow about breaking his hip in Mexico because he knew it would look bad for him if he told the truth. Or maybe he was trying to protect Billy Taylor. Buck said he thought Billy was wanted for something.

I promised Buck I wouldn't ask any more questions, but that was before I heard about D. B. Cooper. I walked back up to the cabin, but when I got there, Buck was gone.

CHAPTER 13

THE JEEP WAS STILL PARKED outside the cabin, but the two-way radio and map were gone and so was Buck's staff. I called his name and searched the area around the cabin, but there was no sign of him. Maybe he got worried and went looking for me. Or, maybe he heard something on the two-way that had to be taken care of right away. I sat on the porch and waited until hunger drove me inside for something to eat.

I put more wood in the stove, dumped a can of chili into the pan, and sat at the table while it heated. I wasn't wearing a watch, but I guessed it was about ten o'clock. Teams one and two would start making their way to the ravine in a few hours.

I got up to stir the chili and the cabin started to shake. I grabbed the pan off the stove before it fell and braced myself against the counter. A plastic plate fell on the floor and rolled next to the locker. The tremor stopped. Minor, I thought, and bent down to pick up the plate. That's when I saw the three padlocks. They were locked together, dangling from a rusty nail hammered into the side of the locker. Pandora's box was unlocked.

I stared at the storage locker trying to remember the story behind Pandora's box. It had something to with a woman named Pandora who had a box that she wasn't supposed to open. Of course, she opened it anyway, releasing a multitude of evils into the world. It was just a myth, I told myself. Buck's locker was exactly what he said it was: a bear-proof storage area.

I lifted the heavy lid expecting to see cases of canned food and other supplies, but what I saw was Buck's walking staff. It was the only thing in the locker. I propped the lid open with a chunk of wood, leaned over, and grabbed the staff. As I pulled it out, the carving of Mount Saint Helens dropped off and fell back into the locker. I thought I had broken it, but when I looked at the top of the staff I saw that the wood was threaded. Sticking up through the center of the staff was a square metal peg, about a half inch across. I climbed into the box and retrieved the mountain peak and screwed it back on. Curious. Was this the reason Buck was so touchy about his staff?

With a flashlight it didn't take long to find the two small, square holes in opposite corners of one end. I put the peg into the first hole and turned the staff. There was a sharp click. When I turned the staff in the second hole, the edge of the floor popped up. Buck's staff was a key. I pulled the trap door open and a gust of cold, rank air hit my face. I reeled backward and almost gagged. It was the same stench we had smelled the first night in the cabin.

Holding my breath, I shined the flashlight down the dark opening. There was a metal ladder that seemed to go down forever. The beam from the flashlight wasn't strong enough to reach the bottom. On the back side of the trap door were two handles. Buck must have climbed down there and latched the door behind him. But why? Where did it lead? There was only one way to find out. I put on my coat and gloves and started down.

The dim light from the cabin faded with each downward step. I was descending into some kind of cavern. The smell seemed to get worse the deeper I went. Finally, my foot touched the ground with a crunch. I didn't know how far the cabin was above me, but it had to be at least two hundred feet. The cavern walls were made out of smooth rock. The ground seemed to be littered with layers of sticks. I bent down for a closer look. Mixed in with the sticks were bones and what looked like shreds of dried animal skin. I shined the flashlight along the wall until it hit a pile of deer and elk antlers as tall as I was.

The word *lair* popped into my brain and my knees started to buckle. I grabbed the ladder to steady myself.

The roaring screams that were waking me at night were not from my dreams. The sounds were real and they had come from here—muffled by tons of rocks. I was standing in the Sasquatch's lair. This is where it ate and took shelter.

I wanted to scramble back up the ladder like smoke going up a chimney, but I didn't. Buck was down here. It was the only place he could have gone. He might be injured or need help.

On the wall across from me were two tunnel openings. I turned the flashlight off for a moment to see if any light came from them. Both openings disappeared in the darkness. I remembered reading that when people saw a Sasquatch in their headlights the animal's eyes reflected light—a sign of nocturnal behavior. The Sasquatch would have to see in the dark like humans see in daylight to live in a place like this.

I turned the flashlight back on. If I called out, Buck would probably be able to hear me, but so would the Sasquatch. Gathering my courage to catch a glimpse of one of them on the trail in daylight was hard enough. I wasn't about to call one to me down here. My only choice was to pick one of the openings and see if it led me to Buck.

I chose the left opening, which led to a long tunnel about six feet wide and ten feet tall. I followed it for two or three hundred feet and stopped. In front of me were four more tunnels. I turned the flashlight off, and again found myself in total darkness. One of the tunnels had to lead outside or how would the Sasquatch get in? But which one?

If I always took the far left tunnels, I would be able to find my way back to the ladder by taking right tunnels. Right? Just in case I was wrong, I found a rock and scraped it along the wall as I walked.

I lost track of how many tunnels I passed through. Some of them were hundreds of feet long, some only a few steps.

After a while all the tunnels started looking the same and I began to wonder if I was going in a circle.

Eventually, I stumbled into a huge cavern, and at first I thought I was back where I started. I was relieved. I had about enough of spelunking. All I wanted was to go up the ladder and eat about six cans of chili. But there was no ladder. And there were no more tunnels. Dead end.

Like the first cavern, the ground was littered with branches and old bones. I was about ready to start retracing my steps, when I heard a now very familiar rumbling, followed a few seconds later by a violent shaking that hurled me to the ground. It was one thing to experience an earthquake above ground, but it's something entirely different to go through one with thousands of tons of rock above your head. It scared me so bad I started to scream, but I couldn't hear myself above the noise of the rattling cave. Rocks pelted me from above like small meteorites. I covered my head and screamed some more and thought my heart was going to burst from my chest.

When the quake finally ended I lay on my back gasping for breath, shocked that I was still alive, and convinced that if it happened again I wouldn't be.

I found the flashlight and started jogging back through the tunnels. But somewhere along the way I screwed up. I reached the end of a tunnel and found a single opening that was too small for me to crawl through.

I started backtracking, desperately looking for my little scrape marks, but all the tunnels I passed through were unmarred.

Panic set in and I began to shout for Buck as I wandered through the tunnels. I no longer cared if the Sasquatch heard me. Maybe one of them could show me how to get out of here.

My voice echoed back to me from all directions. I

don't know how long I wandered around yelling like this, but pretty soon my voice was gone and the shouts were more like whispers.

I stumbled into another large cavern and discovered a very important clue about Buckley Johnson's past.

What are two of the most worthless items you can find when you're lost in a cave? A parachute and two hundred thousand dollars in twenty-dollar bills. There they were, right in my flashlight beam, like a heap of garbage. I collapsed on the pile of bills and closed my eyes.

"I told you it was Pandora's box."

I sat up. Buck was standing above me carrying a lantern. I had never been more happy to see anyone in my whole life. I wouldn't have cared if he had hijacked Air Force One. I threw my arms around him and started crying.

"It's all over now, Dylan. I know the way out of here. You can relax now. It's all over. . . ."

CHAPTER 14

BUT IT WAS FAR from over for either one of us.

I picked up a bundle of bills.

"Does this belong to you?" I asked.

"Not exactly," Buck said.

I told Buck about my conversation with Agent Crow. When I finished, Buck took a deep breath and let it out slowly. "There's a lot more to it than Crow knows. Gary was dying and there was nothing anyone could do about it, he was just wasting away. I read about this new experimental treatment for cancer in Mexico. I wanted to take him down there and see if they could do something for him, but I didn't have the money, and of course my insurance wouldn't pay for it. I couldn't just sit by without doing everything possible for my boy. So, I hijacked the airplane. It might have worked, too, if I hadn't broken my hip when I landed."

"And that's when Billy Taylor found you."

Buck shook his head. "I mean Billy nursed me back

to health, that part's true, but it was a Sasquatch that found me that night. She picked me up and carried me to Billy's."

"She?"

"Yep. A big beautiful female Sasquatch."

"And she *carried* you to Billy's cabin?"

Buck chuckled. "Like a baby. She must have spotted my chute coming down because when I landed she was there within minutes. Seeing her scared me worse than jumping out of that jet. When she picked me up I passed out.

"I woke up in Billy's cabin and thought I had dreamed the whole thing. It wasn't until I saw Billy standing in front of the cabin with the Sasquatch that I knew I had been rescued by a cryptid."

"How long did you stay at the cabin?"

"Weeks. The police and the National Guard were scouring the woods for D. B. Cooper and I couldn't leave. Billy called Betty and told her he had me in the cabin. She asked him to hide me until it was clear. Billy had the perfect hiding spot."

"The cavern below Pandora's box."

"Yep. I stayed down in that miserable hole for two weeks, then he brought me up to the cabin."

"And Gary?"

"He died while I was at Billy's. The treatment in

Mexico probably wouldn't have worked anyway. The only real regret I have about the whole thing was that I wasn't there for Betty when she needed me and I didn't get to say good-bye to Gary. . . ."

A tear glistened on Buck's cheek in the dim lantern light. It was several minutes before he could continue. He took a handkerchief out and wiped his face. "Anyway . . . when I got back home, I wanted to turn myself in, but Betty wouldn't hear of it. She said that she had lost her son and she wasn't about to lose her husband, too. She's the one that concocted the Mexican hit-and-run story. I didn't think the story would fly for a second. I went along with it to humor her. When they hauled me in for that lineup I figured that was it. Someone was bound to pick me out, but they didn't."

"And the money has just sat here all this time?"

"Right where Billy stashed it."

"Agent Crow said that they found some of the money in 1980."

"A few packets fell out of the bag when I was hanging onto the back of that 727. They must have landed in a stream and made their way to the Columbia."

"When did Agent Crow come back into the picture?"

"A few years ago." Buck smiled. "When he first came back, I was scared to death. But I've gotten used to having him around."

157

"You're kidding."

"Seriously. It keeps us both on our toes. How did he look?"

"Terrible."

"He needs to eat better food and exercise, which reminds me. Are you hungry?"

"Starving."

Buck reached into his pocket and brought out a carrot. It wasn't exactly what I had in mind, but it tasted pretty good.

"What is this place?"

"Lava tubes. They're formed when lava on the surface cools and hardens but the molten lava below continues to flow. If it weren't for these tubes, the Sasquatch would have been discovered a long time ago. They spend their days underground and leave the tubes at night to hunt."

"Why did you come down here?"

"I talked to your dad."

"How did—"

"Not in person. On the radio."

"But the others . . ."

"Before he left we set up a code. If he needs to talk to me he'll say something like, 'I just flushed twelve grouse.' Which, means I'm supposed to switch the radio to channel twelve and we can talk without the others hearing us."

"How was he? What's going on?"

"He's tired and worried, which is why he called in. He thinks Kurt Skipp is onto something. Early this morning, Kurt took off on his own and your dad hasn't seen him for hours."

"Where did he go?"

"That's the problem—your dad doesn't know. He says that Kurt is like some kind of wolf. He goes all day, doesn't say a word, doesn't get tired, sleeps about four hours, then takes off again.

"I came down here to make sure everything was okay. There's a surface entrance in that ravine the triplets are poking around in. If they find it the Sasquatch will no longer be a myth."

"Did you tell Dad I was here?"

"No. I think he has enough on his mind right now."

I was relieved he didn't tell him. "What's Dad going to do?"

"He'll know more this evening after they have their powwow. He didn't want to stay on the radio very long, so that's all I know."

"I'm glad you found me. I was scared half to death."

"I'm awful sorry about that, Dylan. I didn't think it would take me so long to get down to the ravine and back. In the old days I used to be able to do it pretty quick. Guess I'm getting too old for this. I also didn't think you'd figure out what the staff is used for. When we heard you yelling after that quake we started looking for you."

"What do you mean—we?"

He smiled pointed out into the dark cavern. "I guess I should have introduced you."

My breath caught in my throat. Standing off in the shadows, near the tunnel opening, was a massive figure. I couldn't see it very clearly, but it had to be at least seven feet tall.

"Don't make any sudden moves," Buck said. "They're real skittish, especially around strangers."

"What's he doing out there?"

"Probably wondering what you're doing here. He's harmless. When you started yelling he led me right to you."

The Sasquatch moved further back into the shadows as if he knew we were talking about him.

"I would have never found you on my own," Buck continued in a quiet voice. "The echoes down here are really confusing, and you kept moving. But it didn't take long for the Sasquatch to hone in on the real thing. They're amazing creatures—powerful, intelligent, and incredibly perceptive. I don't believe in that mental telepathy hocus-pocus, but if any creature has that ability it's the Sasquatch. They always seem to show up at the right time."

I couldn't believe that I was actually looking at a Sasquatch. It was no more than twenty feet away. I wanted to walk over and touch it. Make sure it was real. "Can you talk with them?" I whispered.

"Not talk. They don't have what I would call a vocabulary, but we can communicate after a fashion. Billy was much better than I am. He used hand signs. I wished I could have spent more time up here with him learning how he did it, but he died before I got the chance."

The Sasquatch started moving toward the tunnel. "Where's it going?"

"Hard to say."

Just as the Sasquatch moved through the opening it turned its head and looked back at us. I saw its face clearly. Its large eyes were dark and almond shaped. The hair on its head was much longer than the hair on its body.

"Thanks," I said and it quickly disappeared down the tunnel. "I can't believe this."

"Fortunately for the Sasquatch, very few people believe in them. It's the only thing that has kept them alive all these years."

I stared at the passageway hoping that the Sasquatch would reappear. Buck went on to explain that he had checked out the surface entrance in the ravine.

"I think these earthquakes have opened it up a little more. I suspect the Sasquatch were down there trying to disguise the entrance. They're pretty good at this. Clyde must have heard them working. You would almost have to fall in the entrance to find it, but I'm worried that Clyde or one of his brothers might stumble across it, or worse, convince Flagg to send everyone down there to look. If Kurt Skipp is as good as they say he is, he might be able to find it."

"So, what can we do about it?"

"I've been thinking about that. Come on, I'll show you."

I followed Buck down several tunnels. We came into another cavern. Next to one wall was a pile of huge footprint castings. I picked one of them up. The sole was made out of rubber. Across the top was a strap to attach it to your shoe.

"Where did these come from?"

"I made them a few years back. I took castings of real Sasquatch prints then made molds out of the castings. They leave a pretty convincing Sasquatch print. I'd be surprised if Kurt Skipp could tell the difference between this and the real thing."

They were heavy. "I still don't understand what you use them for. Why would you want to leave fake footprints?"

"Billy used them to get people away from the surface entrances. When searchers got too close, he would go ten or twenty miles away, then call in the footprint discovery anonymously and the Sasquatch searchers would come running.

"Dr. Flagg and his gang would follow Sasquatch footprints across molten lava. I was hoping you would put a pair of these on and lead the expedition away from the ravine."

"Me?"

Buck slapped his bad hip. "I'm afraid my footprints come out a little uneven these days."

The first thing we did when we got back into the cabin was eat. After this we went outside and Buck gave me Sasquatch walking lessons.

"Big strides," he encouraged me. "Giant steps. And don't be afraid of really slamming those footprints down into the ground."

Hopping around with the heavy footprint strapped to my feet was exhausting, and it was going to be a lot harder doing it in the woods when it was dark.

"We won't know where to lay the prints, until your dad contacts us," Buck explained. "He said he would try to slip away and give me a call sometime tonight after they get together."

My lesson was interrupted by the two-way radio.

"I scared up four deer on the way over here," Dad said.

It was great to hear his voice. Buck switched the frequency to channel four. We waited for ten minutes and nothing happened. "Why doesn't he call us?" I asked.

"I don't know. He might have just been telling us the channel for later."

Several more minutes passed, then we heard Joe's voice . . . *"I don't care, Flagg! We don't care! We're leaving now."*

"I wish you would reconsider, Joe," Flagg said.

"I thought they were at the ravine together," I said. "Why are they using the radio? And a different channel?"

"Your dad is holding the send key down on his radio, so we can hear the conversation. Shhh . . ."

"You're going to lose your investment, Joe," Flagg said smoothly. *"You all signed a contract. If you back out now, you won't get a share."*

"Doesn't do a lot of good if we're dead," Henry said. *"That last quake did it for me. I want to find a Sasquatch but not if I have to die to do it."*

"Where's Kurt Skipp?" Clyde asked.

"He's onto something," Flagg said. *"He wanted to check it out before he came in."*

"Nice try, Flagg," Henry said.

"I'm serious."

"Did he see footprints?" Clyde asked.

"No," Dad said. *"He just said he would catch up with us later."*

I could just see Dr. Flagg glaring angrily at Dad. Buck laughed.

"*Doesn't matter if he's onto something or not,*" Joe said. "*It'll be dark in half an hour and I'm not spending another night on this mountain. We're going back to the truck. We're outta here.*"

"Three down," Buck said. "Five to go. Maybe they'll move away from the ravine and you won't have to lay those prints."

"*We'll have to split up tomorrow,*" Flagg said, "*in order to cover the search area.*"

"*We're not done with the ravine,*" Clyde said stubbornly.

There was a long pause, then Flagg said, "*I'll tell you what I'll do. We'll all go down there first thing tomorrow morning. If we don't find anything by noon, we'll continue our sweep through this area. Would that be all right, Clyde?*"

"*Yeah, I guess so.*"

Buck groaned. "Looks like we're going back down into Pandora's box." He switched the radio to the teams' frequency in case Kurt Skipp checked in.

CHAPTER 15

"WE'RE GOING TO LEAD THEM right out of there," Buck said. "I'll take you to the surface entrance. It's right next to the stream that runs along the bottom of the ravine. When you get there, follow the stream for about two miles, then strap on those big feet.

"I want you to jump in and out of the stream like you're trying to catch fish. The Sasquatch do this all the time. Follow that stream right up the hillside and out of that ravine. There's a logging road up on top. Just keep following it until you see me. I'll meet you there in the Jeep. While you're making your way there I'll stomp around with another set of footprints in a new area. They'll think there are two Sasquatch and I guarantee they'll forget about that ravine for the time being."

"How do you know they'll see the footprints in the ravine?"

"S.W.A.G."

"Scientific-Wild-Ass-Guess," I added.

"The easiest way down to the ravine is to cross the stream. Don't worry they'll see them. If they . . ."

"*Johnson?*" The two-way radio barked from the kitchen table. "*Are you out there, Johnson?*" Buck snatched the radio off the seat.

"It sounds like Agent Crow," I said.

"It is! What's he doing? He'll ruin everything!"

"*Batteries are going dead on this thing . . .*" The transmission started to break up. "*I've run off the road near Longmire spur. Guess I was knocked out for a . . . I think my leg is bro . . . I hope . . .*"

"*Are you still out there, Joe?*" Flagg asked. "*Did you catch any of that?*"

"*Some of it,*" Joe said.

"*Who was it?*"

"*I don't know and I don't care. We're at the truck now and we're leaving.*"

"*Was he talking about Buckley Johnson?*" Flagg asked. "*You think he's out here somewhere?*" No one answered. "*Joe?*"

"What time did Agent Crow head back to his car?" Buck asked.

"I saw him about ten o'clock."

Buck looked at his watch. "The only reason that fool's up here is because of me. I have to help him."

"What about the footprints?"

"I'll lead you to the surface entrance, then come back, get the Jeep, and see what I can do for Crow. You take the radio."

"What about you?"

"I'll use Crow's radio when I get to him. We'll use channel four. That way we'll be able to hear your dad if he has any more news for us."

We climbed down into the cavern. Buck led me effortlessly through a bewildering series of tunnels. I wouldn't be able to find my way out of there on my own in a million years. We didn't see any Sasquatch and I was kind of disappointed.

"Here we are," Buck said, leading the way down yet another tunnel. It led to what looked like an underground lake. Water dripped down from the ceiling of the cavern like rain.

"What is this?"

"Lava Lake. At least that's what I call it. The surface entrance is on the other side."

"Do I swim?"

"No, no . . . I have a boat." I followed him to the edge of the water. A small dinghy was tied up there. "Just paddle straight across. You'll see what looks like a set of stairs. They lead up to the entrance. I'd take you across, but I should probably get back to the Jeep. Crow didn't sound . . ."

"I can do this. Go ahead. I'll be fine."

"Okay. Remember, follow the stream for a couple of miles before you put on the big feet. I'll see you on that logging road somewhere. And keep your eyes open for Kurt Skipp. With any luck he's back at camp, but you never know."

Buck hobbled back into the tunnel and I got in the dinghy and started across the lake. I had no problem finding the stairs on the other side. They went up for about twenty feet. On the top was a tunnel and as soon as I stepped into it, I knew it led outside. I could smell the beautiful fresh air! The outside entrance was right behind a waterfall. No one would be able to find it unless they saw a Sasquatch go into it.

I started following the stream, detouring around several beaver ponds. It was rough going in the dark. I used my flashlight sparingly, afraid someone might see it from the top of the ravine. Buck hadn't mentioned how I would know when I had traveled two miles. All I could do is guess. I strapped on the prints and started playing Bigfoot.

After a while I could barely lift my feet. I had to stop and rest. I shined the flashlight on my back trail and I was pleased with what I saw. Sasquatch footprints leave quite an impression in soft sand and an even bigger impression in the minds of those who see them. I started again, but I didn't get very far.

"Buck . . ." It was Dad! *"I don't know if you can hear me or not. But something is definitely going on. Kurt Skipp didn't return to camp, so he must be onto something. I think he might be down in the ravine. I'm on my way down there to see if I can do anything. Clyde says he couldn't pick up radio signals down there, so I guess I'll have to check with you after I get back on top. . . ."*

I stared at the radio. I didn't know if I should tell him I was down there or not.

"Go ahead and answer him, Dylan."

I nearly jumped out of my footprints. A bright light shined in my face.

"Myyyy, what big feet you have," Kurt Skipp said. His flashlight was taped to the top of his rifle. He pointed it along my trail, then back at me. "You've been busy."

I was too stunned to speak.

"Where's Buck?" he asked.

"I don't know who you're talking about."

"Really? Well, I heard this very interesting conversation over the radio this afternoon. It was between Buck and your father. Buck seemed very concerned about this ravine. He told your father that it was imperative that they get us away from this area."

I guess Kurt had broken Dad's radio code. I pressed the send button on the radio, hoping Dad would hear us.

"So, I came down here for a look," Kurt continued. "I didn't see anything, and I was about ready to head back to camp and discuss this with Dr. Flagg, when I heard you crashing around down here."

"So, what are you going to do now?"

"I think we should head up stream together. I'd like to see where you came from. Maybe Buck is there . . . maybe something else. You can take those footprints off. I don't think you'll need them anymore."

I sat down and undid the straps. I slipped the radio into my coat pocket and continued to press the send button.

"You lead," Kurt said.

We started walking along the stream. My only hope was to lead him past the waterfall and out the other end of the ravine. "This whole Bigfoot thing was all a hoax," I said. "Dad and Buck and me were all in on it. Dad's writing a book on hoaxes and this was part of his research."

"Nice try, Dylan." Kurt didn't seem convinced.

"Did you know my dad told Clyde where to take that photo of Sasquatch?"

"So?"

"So, it wasn't a Sasquatch. It was Dad in a gorilla suit, but Clyde didn't know it."

A gust of wind blew an unpleasant smell our way.

"Hold it," Kurt said. "What is that? Smells like a dead animal."

Not now, I thought. We were standing next to a beaver pond. I turned around. Kurt was sniffing the air. Suddenly he stopped sniffing and became very still. He was looking at something just over my shoulder. "You're a liar, Dylan," he said quietly.

I turned to look. The Sasquatch was standing near a big fir tree, not fifty feet away. When I turned back Kurt had raised his rifle. I charged into him. The rifle went off as we fell to the ground. Kurt hit me in the face, then slammed me in the stomach with his knee. I couldn't breathe. He found his rifle and stood up.

"Dylan, I'll come back and deal with you in a minute. But first, I have some business to take care of with your friend."

He started to walk away and I twisted around trying to see if the Sasquatch had gone. A bright light flashed in the sky. Kurt stopped in midstep and looked up. There was a loud hiss, a blast of hot air, then the forest started to come apart.

CHAPTER 16

THE IMPACT OF THE EXPLOSION threw me into the pond. I dove underwater and held my breath for as long as I could. When I popped to the surface for air, I got a mouth full of hot ash. I gagged and went back under. I struggled out of my coat, put it above my head, and surfaced again. The coat protected my head from the hot ash, and I was able to breathe after a fashion.

Trees crashed down all around me, the ground shook, and thunder cracked. I don't know how long I stayed in the icy water. Eventually the noise diminished, then stopped altogether. The only thing I heard were my teeth chattering. I was freezing. I lifted the coat from my head. It was dark out, and there was still a lot of ash in the air, but it looked as if the worst had passed. I stumbled out of the stream. I had to get out of these wet clothes and get dry.

"Dylan? Dylan are you out there . . ." It was Dad. "I don't know if you can hear me. . . ."

The radio. I found it near Kurt Skipp, or what was left of him. He had been crushed by a tree.

"Dad? I'm here! Are you okay?"

"No . . . I'm in bad shape . . . It's good to hear you, Son. I tried to get to you, but the mountain . . ."

"Where are you?"

"I want you to get out of here, Dylan," he said weakly. *"You need to find a road that can be seen from the air. As soon as it gets light they'll send in rescue crews. They'll pick you up. But you have to get . . ."*

"Where are you, Dad?"

"Is Kurt Skipp with you?"

"He's dead. Where are you?"

"You'll need to get out on your own then . . ." He started coughing. *"I'm near a waterfall . . . Don't worry about me. I'll be fine, just get to a road . . ."*

"Dad? Dad . . . ?"

I felt around until I found Kurt's rifle. The flashlight taped to it was still working. I took it off and started toward the waterfall.

I climbed over and under scores of fallen trees. My eyes were swollen and the air was choked with ash, which made it difficult to breathe.

When I got to the falls, I called out for Dad, but he didn't answer. It took me a half an hour to find him. He was slumped next to a tree trunk, unconscious. His breathing was shallow and labored, and when I shook him, he didn't respond. He had hot ash burns all over his face and hands, and there was a deep gash on his forehead, oozing blood. I found a first-aid kit in his pack and wrapped the wound. I needed to find help for him, but first I had to get him out of the ash-filled air so he could breathe easier. I started dragging him to the waterfall. He came to for a moment when the water from the falls hit his face.

"Forget about me, Dylan. You need to get out of here . . ."

"We both need to get out of here," I said, but he didn't hear me because he had passed out again.

I pulled him through the passageway behind the falls and laid him near the edge of Lava Lake. The air inside the cave was clear of ash, and Dad's breathing seemed to improve. Now what? I would never be able to find my way to the cabin through the maze of tunnels. This left going back out to the ravine and hiking to the logging road that Buck had told me about. I wasn't strong enough to drag Dad all the way, which meant I would have to bring help to him. So, after all our efforts to conceal the Sasquatch I was now going to lead people through the cryptid's front door? It wasn't fair, but there didn't seem to be any other choice. Maybe Dr. Flagg was right after all. There just wasn't any more room for the Sasquatch to remain a myth.

Dad's sleeping bag was in his pack. I laid it out and got him into it. There was also a plastic tarp in the pack. I found some sticks and set up a shelter to keep the dripping water from the ceiling off of him. I stripped out of my wet clothes and put on some of Dad's dry clothes, which was a huge relief, then I gathered a pile of sticks and started a small fire to keep Dad warm while I was gone.

Just as I was about to leave I heard a splashing noise from the other side of the lake. At first I thought it must be Buck! That he had found Agent Crow, taken him to the cabin, and had then come down here to look for me.

I shined the flashlight across the lake. It wasn't Buck. It was a Sasquatch, and he was wading toward us. He stopped and shielded his eyes from the light. I lowered the beam to the surface of the water and the Sasquatch continued across the lake. I didn't know if this was the same one that had been with Buck, but it was just as big. The water in the middle of the lake came to his waist. I told myself that there was nothing to be afraid of, that the Sasquatch was harmless, but my heart was beating like a hummingbird's wings. I wanted to run away, but I couldn't leave Dad. The Sasquatch came out of the lake and shook the water of his fur like a dog.

A terrible stench filled the air. The Sasquatch stood on the shore and looked at us for a few moments, then walked over to the fire and squatted down near Dad. He bent over and looked at Dad's face, then gently touched the bandage on his forehead.

I wondered if this was the same Sasquatch that had built the shelter for Dad. Maybe he recognized him.

"He's hurt," I said. The Sasquatch turned his head and looked at me. He may not have understood what I said, but I was certain that he understood that Dad was in trouble.

He stood up and walked toward the stairs leading to the surface entrance.

"Where are you going?"

He paused and glanced back at me, then continued into the passageway. I followed him. When I got outside, he was standing near the waterfall peering into the darkness. The air was still dense with ash. I shined my flashlight over the jumble of fallen trees. If I was going to get help for Dad in time, I had to get moving. With all the fallen trees, the climb out of the ravine was going to be difficult.

The Sasquatch stepped back behind the waterfall. I followed him. I wasn't worried about leaving Dad with the Sasquatch, but I was very worried about the Sasquatch being in the cavern when I returned with help. Leading people to the cavern was bad enough. I didn't want to introduce them to the Sasquatch.

Back inside, the Sasquatch squatted down again and took a close look at Dad's face, then slipped his arms underneath the sleeping bag and stood up with him.

"What are you doing? This is the best place for him right now." I pointed to the ground. "There's no ash in here." I waved my hands in the air. "He can breathe in here." I took an exaggerated breath and let it out.

The Sasquatch paid no attention and started walking across the lake with Dad cradled in his arms. All I could do was follow. I got into the dinghy and paddled across.

When we reached the other side the Sasquatch carried Dad down the tunnel.

After a while I started to recognize some of the tunnels and realized where the Sasquatch was going. He was taking Dad to the cabin.

When we got to the ladder, I shouted for Buck, hoping that he and Agent Crow had somehow gotten back to the cabin. There was no answer. The Sasquatch laid Dad down and made a motion for me to go up the ladder.

"You want me to go first?"

I started up, hoping he understood that I wanted him to bring Dad up behind me. With Dad in the cabin, I could close Pandora's box before I got help. I'd tell the rescuers that we were staying at the cabin when the volcano erupted. The secret of the lava tubes would be safe.

Other than a couple chairs being turned over, and broken dishes on the floor, the cabin was in good shape. I lit a lantern and set it near Pandora's box. Dad's head and shoulders came up through the opening. He was still unconscious. I grabbed him under the arms and pulled him the rest of the way into the box. I checked to see if he were still breathing, and was relieved to see that he was.

The Sasquatch had a difficult time getting his wide, muscular shoulders through the opening, but he managed to wiggle through. He climbed out of the box, then reached over and picked Dad up.

"You can lay him here." I pointed at one of the cots.

The Sasquatch started towards the front door.

"No," I said. "He'll be comfortable right here."

The Sasquatch opened the front door and walked outside.

I followed him. "Where are you going?"

He looked back at me, then continued walking. I wasn't about to try and wrestle Dad away from him. I ran back inside, closed the trap door, turned the locks with the staff, then slammed the lid to Pandora's box. Before I left the cabin, I screwed the carving of Mount Saint Helens back onto the top of the staff and hid it under the sleeping bag on Buck's cot.

I didn't know where the Sasquatch was taking Dad, but he seemed to know where he was going. I followed him down the steep road that led to the cabin. The eruption hadn't done much damage to this part of the mountain and there was less ash in the air. We only had to climb over a few trees on our way down the hill.

When we got to the main road I remembered I still had Kurt's radio. I tried to reach Buck, but there was no response. I switched channels and tried the team frequency, expecting the same results, but Dr. Flagg answered immediately . . .

"Who is this?"

"Dylan Hickock. Are you okay?

"Broken arm, but I'll live. What are you doing up here?"

"I came up to find Dad."

"He's not here . . . I'm alone."

"Where's Clyde and his brothers?"

"We heard a shot last night and they ran down into this ravine we were searching. That's the last time I saw them. I don't know where your dad and Kurt are either . . ."

I didn't tell him that Dad was with me. He would probably want to talk to him and it would be hard to explain why he couldn't.

"I'm on my way down the mountain," I said. "Where are you?"

"I'm above that ravine. It's between roads 626 and 628."

"I'll send someone. Just wait there."

"*Dylan . . .*"

I wasn't in the mood to talk to Dr. Flagg. I turned the radio off.

The sun rose, casting a strange reddish light through the ashy air. Large sections of forest had been flattened by the blast. The downed trees looked like gray tooth-picks spilled on the hillsides.

We walked for miles. Actually, I jogged most of the time—the Sasquatch was hard to keep up with. When I got too far behind he would stop and wait for me. There was no change in Dad's condition, but at least he was alive. We reached a paved road and I began to wonder if the Sasquatch was going to carry Dad right into the near-est town.

He didn't have to. About a mile down the road the Sasquatch came to a sudden stop. He looked up at the sky as if he were listening to something. I couldn't hear anything. He set Dad on the ground. Then I heard it, and a few seconds later, saw it. A helicopter, flying low to the ground, appeared from behind the hill in front of us. I jumped up and down and started yelling. It hov-ered for a second, sending up clouds of swirling ash, then landed in the middle of the road.

Two men jumped out of the chopper and ran over to us.

"I'll get the stretcher," one of them said and ran back for it.

The second man looked around curiously. "I thought there were three of you?"

I looked around, too. The Sasquatch had vanished.

"No," I said. "Just my dad and me."

AFTER...

DAD REGAINED CONSCIOUSNESS later that day. I was sitting next to his hospital bed. His first words were . . .

"Did they find it?"

"No. The Sasquatch are safe . . . for now."

He smiled and closed his eyes. The doctors said he was going to be fine but he would have to stay in the hospital for awhile. Some of the burns he had were pretty bad and the hot ash had damaged his lungs.

Joe West, Henry, and Dean made it off the mountain without a scratch. I saw them being interviewed on the television from the hospital room. They said they had been fishing when the mountain erupted.

Dr. Theodore Flagg was also interviewed. He said he was on the mountain looking for Sasquatch and was going to write a book about his experience during the eruption. He was treated at the same hospital as Dad, but he never came by to see how Dad was doing.

Clyde and his brothers were never seen again. Maybe

he found that gate to Zona after all.

They found what was left of Buck's Jeep on a logging road, but Buck wasn't in it. There was no sign of Agent Crow's Taurus. The area he had gone off the road was one of the worst hit areas on the mountain.

I went to the hospital every day to visit Dad, then went to Buck's and knocked on his door, hoping he would answer He wasn't home, and I knew he wasn't coming home. I was really going to miss him.

It took me a week to get a hold of Mom in Egypt. I told her Dad was in the hospital. I didn't tell her why we had been on the mountain. I thought I should leave that to Dad. The eruption on Mount Saint Helens was going to seem like a belch, when she found out what we were doing up there.

The night before her return I found this E-mail message on my computer:

An old friend is coming by for a visit tonight at 8 P.M.
Buck :)

I read this message a dozen times and still couldn't believe it had come from Buck! At eight o'clock a car pulled into the driveway. I opened the front door expecting to see Buck, but it wasn't him.

Agent Crow got out of the backseat of a taxicab. He

was on crutches. I went out to meet him.

"I thought . . ."

He held his hand up and spoke to the driver. "Wait here. I won't be long. Let's go inside, Dylan."

When we got inside he sat down on the sofa.

"I thought you were dead," I said. "I thought Buck and you . . ."

"I thought so, too," he said. "He found me just before the mountain erupted. When it blew he jumped into the front seat and we were buried under tons of trees. The doors wouldn't open. I know that. I kept drifting in and out of consciousness. Every time I came to he told me we were going to be just fine, but I knew he was lying. We were dead men.

"I don't know how long we sat there like that. I have a vague memory of hearing logs being moved and metal grinding as the door was being pried opened. The next thing I know I'm lying on the road and Buck's standing above me waving at the sky. I have no idea how he got us out of that car."

I had a very good idea. He had a little help from his friends.

"They flew us out and took us to the hospital. Buck was released the next day."

"How long were you down there before Buck found you?"

"Most of the day. I went off the road right after I saw you. According to the doctors I had a heart attack. Can you believe that?"

Easily, I thought. "So, where's Buck?"

"I have no idea. I just got out of the hospital half an hour ago. The nurse said that a man asked her to give me these." He reached into his pocket and came out with a set of keys that looked familiar. "She said the man told her I should take these over to Dylan's and see if he had a freezer."

I led Agent Crow into the garage. He looked at the freezer for a moment, then slipped on a pair of rubber gloves.

"You better step back, Dylan." I don't know if he expected a bomb or a Sasquatch to jump out. He put the key in, turned the lock, then opened the lid very slowly. "Well, I'll be. Give me a hand."

Inside was a parachute and a big plastic bag filled with bundles of twenty-dollar bills. I helped him pull the bag and parachute out. Underneath them we found Buck's walking staff and two envelopes with our names on them.

Agent Crow opened his first. Inside was a single sheet of paper that read:

I Buckley Johnson confess to the hijacking of Northwest Airlines Flight 305 on the night of November 24, 1971.

Sincerely,

Buckley Johnson, a.k.a. D. B. Cooper

The note addressed to me said:

Dylan,

This is the deed to my cabin. I've signed it over to you and your dad. It's just too much work for an old man like me. The staff is for you. Something to remember me by.

Lava Lake has been closed down. I thought it was best under the circumstances.

Please tell Agent Crow that he needs to start eating better and exercising. It would be a shame if he keeled over before he caught me.

All my Love, Buck

"Are you going to go after him?" I asked.

"Of course," he said. "Like Buck says, I need the exercise."

"What about the money?"

"I'm going to take it down to F.B.I. headquarters right now. Give me a hand."

I helped him haul the bag and the parachute out to the cab. Agent Crow got into the back seat and rolled the window down.

"So, Dylan," he said. "Did you ever see that Sasquatch?"

"In my dreams, Agent Crow. In my dreams."

After he drove away I went back inside. I picked up the staff and saw that Buck had carved a new face into it. I held it under the light. It looked a lot like me.